Murder in the Museum
An Edmund DeCleryk Mystery

by

Karen Shughart

For information, email Cozy Cat Press, cozycatpress@aol.com or visit our website at: www.cozycatpress.com

COZY CAT
PRESS

ISBN: 978-1-946063-50-2

Printed in the United States of America

Cover design by Paula Ellenberger
www.paulaellenberger.com

10 9 8 7 6 5 4 3 2 1

Dedication

This book is dedicated to my husband, Lyle, who is my fiercest supporter, most honest critic and the love of my life; to the memory of my mother, Rennie Green, who was an avid Cozy mystery reader; and to Patricia Rockwell, publisher/editor, for her support.

Acknowledgements

I am not a criminalist, but I've always had a passion for murder mysteries, police procedurals and crime shows on television. This story is completely one of my imagination, but some of the historical information is loosely based on research I did on the history of Lake Ontario and the communities that border it, both in the United States and Canada. While I took some license in describing investigative procedures and other aspects of the book, a number of experts generously provided me with technical advice and answers to my many questions. I can't thank you enough. Any inaccuracies are my fault, not yours.

Dave Phelps, Commander (Retired), Monroe County (NY) Sheriff's Department

Jason Maitland, Lt. (Retired), Rochester (NY) Police Department; Director of Campus Safety and Adjunct Professor at Finger Lakes Community College

Barry C. Virts, Sheriff, Office of the Sheriff of Wayne County, NY

Jeffrey Fosdick, Undersheriff, Office of the Sheriff of Wayne County, NY

Steve Sklenar, Chief Deputy, Police Services, Office of the Sheriff of Wayne County, NY

Sodus Bay Historical Society

And of course, my readers, loving friends and cheerleaders, Mary Quinn, Shelley Usiatynski and Deb Vater, who helped make the book more credible.

Last, but certainly not least, our children Jessica Hurwitz, Jeremy and Debbie-Bux Hurwitz.

PROLOGUE
York, Upper Canada, British North America
1847

He'd been a healer, here in this land so far from where he'd been born, working alongside his beloved wife, administering potions and poultices to villagers who trusted that he'd make them well, or at least ease the discomfort of dying. How different from his beginnings.

While his childhood had been one of loss and sorrow, his life as an adult had been blessed with many riches: a loving family, good neighbors, a land full of bounty. He knew, though, that his time in this welcoming place, his adopted place, would soon end, and before he passed he'd pledged to record his story with the hope that someday someone would discover and read his manuscript, his confession, and right the wrong he'd committed so long ago. He'd lived a good and honorable life, here in this Canadian wilderness, but earlier, many years ago....

He picked up his pen, dipped it in ink and began to write, remembering with clarity the details from his boyhood and the circumstances that had brought him here. He needed to write quickly. Just after dawn, his wife had left him to visit with their daughter, who lived in a nearby village, to help tend to her growing brood of young ones. She would return in time for their evening meal.

Many hours later he sealed the pot of ink, wiped his pen, and after the ink had dried, closed the chamois-bound manuscript. Placing it in a metal box, he removed a large, loose stone from the fireplace hearth, set the box into a niche he had carved, and replaced the stone. He heard in the distance the clomping of horses' hooves and the clacking wheels of a carriage that after a few minutes stopped in front of their simple stone cottage. He peered out the small casement window in their front parlor. His wife had arrived. He heard the door open.

"My dear," he beamed as he opened his arms to embrace her. "I trust the grandchildren are well, and that your day was pleasurable."

PART ONE
Chapter 1
Lighthouse Cove, New York
This century

Annie DeCleryk, executive director of the Lighthouse Cove Historical Society and Museum, saved her document in a Word file, backed it up on a flash drive, pushed her chair away from her desk, and stood up and walked to the kitchen to make herself a cup of tea. Filling the tea kettle with water, she placed it on a burner of the old gas stove and turned the burner on. After pulling a large, brown speckled, glazed ceramic mug from a cupboard, she went into the pantry where she took a tin from a shelf, opened it and pulled out a bag of spiced black tea, one of her favorites.

A few minutes later she was stretched out on the living room sofa reading a mystery, the steaming mug, redolent with cinnamon and cloves, in hand; her ten-year-old beagle, Gretchen, snuggled up against her. It was late afternoon on a gray day in November, and a warming fire crackled in the fireplace. She'd just finished reading a chapter and had placed the half-drunk cup of tea on the coffee table when she heard the backdoor open.

"Hi, Annie, I'm home," her husband, Ed, called out. Hearing his voice, Gretchen jumped off the sofa and ran, white-tipped tail up and wagging, to eagerly greet the retired Lighthouse Cove, New York police chief who'd spent the past few days working as a criminal consultant in a small town located in New York's southern tier near the Pennsylvania border.

Ed petted Gretchen, scratched her ears, then walked into the living room, the dog dancing and jumping at his side. Annie, a small woman with short, tousled salt and pepper hair, rose from the sofa to greet him. She was dressed in trim dark blue jeans and a tunic-length cornflower-blue cashmere turtleneck sweater that matched the color of her eyes. Standing on her tiptoes, she gave her tall, lanky, white-haired spouse a hug and a kiss.

"I'm glad you're back. I missed you. How'd everything go?"

"I missed you, too." Ed beamed as he and his wife kissed again. "It went well, and the police chief is pleased. His detectives caught the murderer across the border in Pennsylvania this morning, and during the few days preceding the capture I worked with him to develop some investigative procedures that will help close cases in the future without having to hire an outside consultant.

"That force is even smaller than ours, and since the closest city is a hundred miles away, they don't have easy access to forensic technologists like we do when a violent crime happens. Sorry I didn't call, but by the time we finished up each evening, it was pretty late."

"That's fine. I appreciated your texts each morning. What's your next project?"

"I don't have one. Since it's so close to Thanksgiving, I decided that I'm not going to take on any more consulting jobs until after the holidays. As you know, I've been working non-stop for almost a year. I need a break and want to start acting like I'm really a retired guy," Ed responded with a smile.

"As if you could," laughed Annie. "What do you plan to do as a," she held up the index and middle fingers on both hands to form an air quote, "retired guy?"

"I have plenty to do," Ed huffed, acting wounded. But his sapphire blue eyes gleamed with amusement. "I want to work on restoring the antique boat that's been sitting in the garage since last summer and the Datsun 280Z that's been there almost as long as we've owned this house. I also plan to get my metal detector out and do some exploring along the beach before the snow comes; I'm thinking I might even do that tomorrow morning. And I want to have lunch with my Navy buddies and enjoy the holidays with you and our family."

"Sounds ambitious," Annie responded with a tolerant smile, knowing full well that her husband of 40 years couldn't possibly accomplish all he intended before the holidays or during the next year, for that matter.

Ed changed the subject. "What did you do while I was away? Did you work or take a little time for yourself for a change?"

Annie smiled. "I worked, but not too hard. I finally completed the brochure on the history of Lighthouse Cove I've been writing so I'll have it ready for tourist season. You know me, I wordsmith everything I write to death, but I'm at the point where it's good enough. I started with when French and Dutch settlers came here after the Revolution and continued to the present. I also included information about shipwrecks since we know that pirates sank ships in these waters beginning in the 1600s."

"Wasn't there also a converted British warship that disappeared in the late 1700s?"

"There was. It was called the HMS Orion, but pirates didn't sink it. It was on its way from New York to Canada when it capsized during a horrible storm. All who were aboard drowned, including some members of Great Britain's royal family. It was rumored they were carrying valuable trinkets to be presented to the Canadian governor of York.

"Divers found what was left of it during an expedition a century later, but they only found bits of the ship's wreckage, some old coins, dish shards and a few skeletal remains, which because there was no way to scientifically identify them back then, were left to molder at the bottom of the lake and never returned to England."

"Sounds interesting. I'd like to read it. Do I have time before dinner?" Annie nodded.

"Good. But first I want to go upstairs and change. In the meantime, why don't you pour us each a glass of wine," Ed requested.

A short while later Annie, humming an oldies' song from the 1960s, put the remaining touches on their dinner: a spicy fish chowder; coleslaw with a tangy oil and vinegar dressing and hard, crusty, sourdough rolls while Ed, dressed in jeans and a red plaid flannel shirt with wine glass in hand, read the brochure.

Annie came into the room just as he was finishing. "So, what do you think?" she asked.

Ed grinned and gave Annie a thumb's up.

"Thanks. I've got to lay it out, insert the artwork, and take it to our printer so we can have it by early spring. Dinner's ready. Let's go eat."

Chapter 2

Emily Bradford, board secretary and head of the gift shop for the Lighthouse Cove Historical Society and Museum, woke up the next morning at about 5 a.m. and couldn't fall back asleep. It was mid-November and still dark, but she decided she'd get dressed and head out early to get some work done before the board meeting started at 9 a.m.

A former professor of creative writing at the University of Rochester, the 48-year-old had taken an early retirement three years ago and relocated to the quaint historic village on the shores of Lake Ontario, hoping the breathtaking scenery and quiet lifestyle would inspire her to create her own literary works rather than teaching others how to do it. She was making progress, and had just signed a deal with a publisher for her first book of poetry.

Still in her nightgown, Emily opened her back door and stepped outside to assess the weather. A scrim of frost was on the grass and the air felt heavy with moisture, but there was no snow, at least not yet. After showering and dressing in a long woolen skirt, turtleneck sweater and high leather boots, the petite woman pulled her glossy shoulder-length hair back and secured it with a velvet band, accentuating her translucent heart-shaped face and wide moss green eyes. She quickly drank a cup of strong black tea infused with milk and a little honey, rinsed the mug and put it in the dishwasher. Carefully cutting the cinnamon streusel coffee cake she'd baked the day before into 12 pieces, she put the plastic lid on the pan and the pan into her canvas tote bag along with her purse, a bottle of water and her cell phone.

After donning a hooded toggle coat, muffler and knitted mittens, she slung the tote bag over her shoulder and headed out into the brisk, frosty air. The wind blowing in from the northeast had picked up. Putting her head down as a buffer against it, she scurried rather than walked the five blocks to the museum, which stood on a bluff overlooking the lake. She heard the crashing thunder of the waves as they slammed against the shoreline and as she looked up at the milky, starless sky she thought there might be snow later that day.

Unlocking the door to the museum, she entered the building, flipped the wall switch for the oversized opaque glass schoolhouse pendant light in the hallway, and went into her tiny office, which adjoined the gift shop to the right of the hall. She turned on the small lamp with a low-watt bulb that was on her desk, feeling calmed by the quiet dimness of the pre-dawn room. After hanging her coat on a hook behind her door and placing her tote bag and purse under her desk, she carried the cake down the hall to the board room where she turned on the floor lamp just inside the room, placed the cake on the sideboard, set up the coffee with a timer to start brewing at 8:30 and then returned to her office.

In addition to completing some paperwork before the meeting, she also wanted to assess what she would need to order for the gift shop when it opened to tourists in May. The posters, photographs and postcards of Lighthouse Cove, provided by a colony of resident artists and photographers, had sold well the past season as had the nautical-inspired gift items, jewelry and locally produced jams, sauces and jellies. Time permitting, she also planned to package some of the jewelry she'd received from orders placed at sales outlets at the end of last season.

She observed that the door to the cellar—its entrance at the back of her office—was slightly ajar. She got up and shut the door, grumbling about drafts in old buildings, and heard a dull, sharp noise just after she sat down at her desk. The furnace system was old and often rumbled and clanked when it first kicked on. The sound distracted her.

As she listened more carefully, the clanking got louder, and she wondered if someone else were in the building. She called out, but by then the noise had stopped, and when no one responded, she shrugged and shook her head.

Nerves again, she thought. Only she, Charles Merrill, the museum's president; Suzanne Gordon, the board treasurer; and the museum director, Annie DeCleryk, had keys, and none of their cars had been in the parking lot when she'd arrived. She shivered as she felt a cold draft on her back from the wind that was whistling through the cracks of the old gray stone building. With a deep sigh, Emily returned to her paperwork, thinking she probably should get up and check to make sure the furnace was still working and that she had locked the front door.

Chapter 3

Ed DeCleryk started out for the beach with his metal detector at 7 a.m. He loved this time, just before dawn, when the village was still quiet. Like Emily, he too had noticed the wind picking up and decided that instead of heading for the wide exposed beach that was closer to his home, he'd walk to the narrow, more sheltered rocky one that lay beneath the bluff where the museum stood. He could see both the bay and the lake as he strolled along the narrow peninsula to his destination and reflected on how the small village had changed since the summer.

Boats that for months had gridlocked the marinas now sat shrink-wrapped in blue plastic, layered like folded sheets on concrete shelves in high and dry facilities. Docks secured in the water behind beach cottages on the bay had been lifted onto land for winter and placed upended, side by side, like oversized sliding boards. Gift shops where tourists stood in line to taste homemade fudge and purchase Lighthouse Cove T-shirts and memorabilia were shuttered, their doors locked and tightly bolted. Picnic tables and benches where families had sat just a few months earlier to enjoy baskets of fried fish and huge cones of homemade ice cream were piled up like flotsam and jetsam against boarded up snack bars.

Gulls awakening from slumber flew up as one mass into the sky, screeching, as Ed approached the beach beneath the bluff. Overhead a squadron of Canada geese, silhouetted low against the horizon, flew southwest towards orchards, vineyards and cornfields where they would forage for food. A bald eagle circled above him. To the east he could see drumlins, deeply etched cliffs carved from glaciers thousands of years before, towering like fortresses against the sea.

Anticipating the damp chill and gusting wind, the lanky 62-year old had pulled on a pair of jeans and slipped an insulated windbreaker over a thick, cotton turtleneck and cable knit sheep's wool sweater. A pair of thermal-lined duck boots protected his feet from the sandy muck and waves that were slowly swallowing up the beach. Ed clomped along, skimming his detector over the sand and rocks, listening for the tell-tale beeping sound that indicated metal nearby. It was hard to hear with the waves pounding against the shore, but the detector went off a couple of times yielding some brass nails, a metal dresser knob, a rusted chain and what appeared to be an old coin. He picked up the coin and put it in his pocket.

As he skimmed it over a greater and wider span of rocks and sand, the detector started beeping again as he neared a stand of tasseled wheat-colored sea-grasses that intermingled with decaying wildflowers clustered together around some boulders against the base of the bluff.

Chapter 4

At 7:15 a.m. the phone rang at the Lighthouse Cove police station. Joe Marion, the dispatcher, took the call and ran to get Ben Fisher, the police chief, who'd been at the station since 6:30 for a meeting with his deputy chief, Carrie Ramos. They were just finishing up when Joe appeared in the doorway of the office and told them that Charles Merrill was on the line and sounded very upset but insisted on speaking only with Ben. Ben, shaking his head, picked up. "Good morning, Charles, what can I do for you?"

Trying unsuccessfully to stay calm, Charles shouted that there had been a break-in at the museum. He told the chief he'd come in early to prepare for the board meeting, finding both front and back doors ajar; artifacts, memorabilia and tourist materials scattered everywhere, and Emily Bradford's coat and scarf hanging on a peg in her office. "I think she was here to start the coffee and to do some work before our board meeting began and must have startled a burglar," he cried. "But she's not here now. What could have happened to her?"

Ben told Charles that he was on his way and instructed him to lock the door and not let anyone, including other board members, into the building. He quickly briefed Carrie, then headed for his patrol car and was just getting into it when Carrie ran out of the station and yelled for him to stop.

"Ed DeCleryk just called from his cell phone. He's found Emily Bradford's body along the base of the bluff beneath the museum. He said he'll stay with her until one of us gets there, but we'll have to move quickly. The wind's picked up, and the water's rising."

Ben closed his eyes and took a deep breath. "That's a terrible shame," he said, then continued, "I need to get to the museum, Carrie, and talk with Charles about the break-in. There's a possibility Emily's death may be related to it. You'll have to go to the beach and meet Ed. Before you go, ask Joe to call Mike Garfield to let him know what's going on and that there's some urgency for him to get to the site to examine the body because of the rising water. Also, please ask Joe to call Dave Burns at the firehouse so he can get his rescue crew to retrieve Emily's body as soon as Mike is finished."

Carrie nodded and ran back inside the police station while Ben turned the lights and sirens on in the patrol car and, tires screeching, raced toward the museum. As he drove, he wondered what was so valuable there that a thief might want to kill for it.

The snow was starting to fall, small, feather-like scattered flurries at first, then heavier and denser until it began to cover the ground. Charles Merrill, trembling from nerves and the cold, thought it might be March before the village would see grass again. As he looked out the front window, the 75-year-old retired University of Toronto professor of archaeology saw Carrie Ramos' and the medical examiner's cars speeding down the road towards the lower end of the beach.

At the same time, the police chief's car and fire rescue truck careened around the corner into the museum parking lot. The burly, mahogany-skinned police chief jumped out of his car and sprinted to the front door, while Dave Burns and two other rescue workers raced towards the bluff with a gurney and some rappelling cables. Charles whispered, "Oh my

God." He had a terrible sense of foreboding as he watched the rescue crew lower the gurney on cables down to the beach.

Chapter 5

The young teacher's car skidded into the school parking lot, now slick with snow, at 7:50 a.m., ten minutes before the bell rang. Despite his best efforts he'd gotten off to a late start.

He hoped his tardiness hadn't been noticed. He'd experienced nausea, dizziness and chills for the past hour but didn't want to take any sick leave this close to Thanksgiving break. Maybe he'd start feeling better as the day progressed. If he kept his mind on his teaching, maybe the symptoms would pass.

He ran to his classroom, quickly pulling his jacket off. As he placed it on the hook behind his door he noticed the cashmere scarf he'd wound around his neck before leaving home was missing. His father had bought and monogrammed it during a trip to Europe in August and gave it to him for his birthday last month.

Damn, he thought, hoping that it had fallen off in his car or in the parking lot during his sprint to get to his classroom and that someone would find it and take it to the office. He'd hate to disappoint his dad by having to tell him he'd lost it, especially since they'd become so close lately. Sliding into the chair behind his desk, he took a deep breath, just as the first of his students started to arrive.

His cell phone vibrated in his pocket. He pulled it out and saw that it was an incoming call from his dad. He didn't have time to answer it so let voice mail pick up. He'd call him back after he got home in the afternoon.

As he put the phone back in his pocket, he noticed that the knees of his khaki pants were smudged, probably when he'd brushed against his dirty car in haste to get to work on time. He grabbed a tissue and wiped them off, then ran his fingers through his unruly hair, praying that the rest of his day would be better than it had started.

Chapter 6

Several hours later, Ed, Ben, and Carrie sat at a table by a window overlooking the roiling lake inside Bistro Louise, a favorite beverage and pastry shop of both locals and tourists, watching the snow come down in blinding, whirling sheets now mixed with icy pellets of frozen rain. By then, most of the villagers had heard about the burglary and Emily's death, and patrons were abuzz with conversation about the tragedy.

"It's a true nor'easter. As we all know, we usually don't get storms of this intensity until after Thanksgiving. We may be in for a very long winter," reflected Ben, a former defense lawyer who had decided he liked solving crimes more than defending the criminals who committed them.

As he drank hot, strong black coffee and munched on an apple fritter, he remarked, "Too bad this storm didn't hold off until we had time to look for clues in the park between the lighthouse and bluff: signs of dragging, blood, pieces of clothing, anything that could help us figure out what happened. With all the snow and ice, that's one avenue that's closed, at least for now. It's amazing you found the body, Ed."

Ed, who'd been drinking a cup of steaming green tea and nibbling on a cinnamon pumpkin scone, put the scone down, brushed the crumbs from his lips and answered, "Dumb luck. If I'd gotten a later start this morning the water would have been so high I wouldn't have walked that stretch of beach because it's so narrow. And if the snow had started earlier, I probably would have put on my hiking boots and gone for a walk in the village park instead of taking my metal detector to the beach."

He took another bite of his scone, chewed and swallowed it and continued, "Emily happened to be wearing jewelry, which is why my detector went off in the first place. If I hadn't discovered her body, given the high winds and rough surf today, she most likely would have been washed out to sea and be considered a missing person, whereabouts unknown."

He asked Ben, "Did Mike estimate the TOD, and does he know how she died?"

"From his preliminary examination, he thinks she was killed sometime between 5:30 and 6:30 this morning," replied Ben, running his fingers through his short, tight, curly black hair.

"The back of her head was bashed in, her neck's broken, she has multiple abrasions and several broken bones, but he won't know what really killed her until he completes the autopsy. There was no evidence of sexual assault." He paused for a few seconds. "Not that that's any consolation."

"So, she could have been beaten to death, killed by the blow to her head, and if her neck's broken, she may have been thrown over the bluff rather than carried down to the beach," Ed concluded.

"Yes, any of those are possibilities, Ed. But if she were thrown over the bluff, it had to have been someone with some strength to do that, although she was tiny, can't have weighed much more than 100 pounds," observed Ben, deep sorrow registering in his dark brown eyes. "Maybe she was taken by surprise and didn't suffer."

"When we moved here I never expected anything like this to happen," Carrie commented, biting into a warm, just out of the oven, homemade chocolate chip cookie. The assistant chief, who had a long, lean body, topaz-colored eyes and shiny light brown hair pulled back into a low ponytail, had worked as a homicide detective in Syracuse but had relocated to Lighthouse Cove to take her current job three years earlier with her husband Matt, a physician now practicing emergency medicine at the local hospital.

"How's Charles holding up?" she asked Ben, taking a sip of steaming hot chocolate.

"As you would expect, he's shaken, and very upset. I found him standing in the foyer, overcoat buttoned up to his chin with his briefcase in hand. His hair was rumpled. He said he'd tripped over the debris and fell when he walked into the museum and dirtied his pants and bruised his knee.

"I asked him if there were family members or friends he could call who'd take him home and stay with him awhile. He informed me he'd never married, and most of his family and close friends still live in Canada.

"He admitted that, other than Annie, the only person he was friendly with on the board was Emily. They had their teaching careers in common, plus he said she'd always been very kind to him. Poor man. He has no idea why anyone would break in and thinks probably Emily's presence caught the burglar by surprise."

"Does he know if anything's missing?" asked Ed.

Ben shrugged. "He doesn't. The place is a mess, and what's odd is that it doesn't look like any locks were picked. The burglar may have had a key, or the door may not have been locked to begin with. Just before I left for the ME's office, the other board members and Annie arrived. Charles was still inside, but as I instructed, he wouldn't let them in. They were all in a state of shock after I explained what happened. I told everyone but Annie to go home but asked that they stay in the village as we'd want to interview them, probably later today.

"I also requested that they voluntarily let us fingerprint them, just to rule them out as suspects. They all want to help find Emily's killer and readily consented."

"Where's Charles now?" asked Ed.

"He's at home. Suzanne Gordon drove to the museum this morning, but Charles walked, and because he was so shaken she offered to take him home and stay with him until he cleaned up and calmed down," replied Ben. "She has a background in mental health so will know all the right things to do and say. She may be with him for hours, so we most likely will be able to interview them at the same time."

Suzanne, tall, with an athletic build, mocha skin, large espresso-colored eyes and dark, corn-row braided hair, ran a wellness center in the village. As a child she, her parents and siblings had emigrated from Jamaica to New York City and then, when she was a teenager, moved to Rochester where her father became the executive chef and partner of the five-star rated Caribbean restaurant, Callaloo.

He continued, "After everyone left, Carrie and I secured the building, and I called the state police and asked that they send some forensic technologists to assist with the investigation. They'll be working with Carrie and Luke Callens, our new detective."

He turned to Ed, "Have you met him?"

Ed nodded. "Yes, a few weeks ago at The Brewery. Annie and I were there for dinner, and he was with our neighbors, Joe and Sue Riley, who introduced us to him."

Ben continued, "Luke's well qualified, and he's going to be a good addition to the force. You should get to know him, you two have a lot in common. Like you, he's a retired SEAL."

"Interesting. We'll have to invite him over for dinner some night. It might be nice to trade stories about the Navy, at least those we can share."

Ben took another sip of coffee and continued, "The techs are at the museum right now with Annie, who's assessing the damage and trying to determine if there are any artifacts missing, but when I left, Luke still hadn't arrived. Carrie, I thought you called to tell him to meet the techs ASAP. Where is he?"

"I did call him. He was running a bit late, I'll tell you why in a minute. He said he'd meet us here once he checked with the techs to make sure they have everything they need. I'll text him to see what's keeping him."

She had just sent the text when Detective Luke Callan walked through the door of the bistro, stamping the snow off his brown tooled leather cowboy boots. The tall, broad-shouldered man shrugged out of his wet parka and hung it on the coat rack just inside the door; brushed wet, white flakes of snow mixed with pearly bits of ice off his short, sandy hair and close-cropped beard; and walked over to the table where the chief, Carrie and Ed were talking. Ed got up, pulled a chair from an empty table and slid it next to him, and Luke sat down, crossing his blue-jeaned legs.

"Morning," the blue-eyed detective said to the group. The young, very pretty, red-haired server approached the table with coffee pot in hand and started to pour coffee into a mug she had placed in front of Luke. He waved her away. "Not this morning, Terri."

"Then how about something to eat?" Terri asked, smiling broadly.

"No thanks, not hungry," he responded, his eyes bleary and face drawn and pale with fatigue. Disappointed, the young woman walked away.

The chief said, "Morning, Luke. You're looking like something the cat dragged in. Too much partying last night after work?"

Luke groaned, "I wish." He said to Carrie, "Didn't you tell him?"

She shook her head. "Just starting to. Go ahead."

Luke sighed and rolled his eyes. "You had already left for the day, Chief, when our rookie, Brad, called in sick, just as the shift was changing." He looked at Ed. "It was the 3:30 to 11:30 p.m. shift."

Carrie added, "In fairness, Brad sounded awful, apparently some stomach bug that started with no warning. There was no way he could come into work yesterday afternoon. Luke and I were just finishing a meeting when he called, and when Luke heard me tell Brad I'd take his shift he offered to take my place, so I could spend the evening with Matt. He's been working nights for a co-worker who's been on maternity leave, and for the first time in weeks he had the evening off. Since I had no idea we'd be investigating a murder today, I told Luke he didn't need to rush into work this morning. He worked about 17 hours yesterday."

"Thanks, Luke," the chief said. "As I think you've already observed, when you're a member of a law enforcement team in a small village, you have to be flexible."

"No problem. I'm fine with it," responded Luke, then pulled a face and rolled his eyes again. The chief cocked an eye at him and, immediately realizing how inappropriate he'd been, Luke apologized.

"Sorry for the grumpiness. I had a lot of coffee during the shift because I wanted to stay alert. Then when the shift ended I was wide awake and very hungry, so I went to Captain Rick's for a burger and a beer and hung out at the bar for a while. I didn't get home until about 1 a.m. and had trouble falling asleep. Too much caffeine, I guess. I didn't even get out for my run this morning. The alarm went off at 5 a.m., but I turned it off, then couldn't fall back asleep right away and had finally dozed off again when Carrie called, so I'm pretty tired."

"Apology noted and accepted," Ben said and then added sympathetically, "and you're going to have a long day today. Unfortunately, there's nothing much that can be done about that." He paused before continuing, "I'm assuming your last drive around the village was about 11:00?" Luke nodded. "Did you notice anything suspicious at the museum or on Peninsula Drive, where Emily lived?"

Luke shook his head. "The village was very quiet, and there were no lights on in the museum when I drove by it. When I drove down Emily's street I noticed that lights were on in a few homes, but most of her neighbors are summer residents or retirees who are gone for the winter, so her street was pretty dark."

"I'd like you to work closely with the techs and Carrie on the investigation, Luke," the chief instructed him. "I went home early yesterday because I needed to deal with a family crisis, and as soon as we're finished here I'll be heading out of town for several days. I know you don't want coffee, but are you sure you don't want something to eat?"

"I'm fine. Thanks."

"Then go ahead back to the museum. Is Annie still there?"

"She is. The techs will be there awhile and will make sure she doesn't contaminate any of the evidence. When I left, she was still assessing the damage and trying to figure out if there's anything missing."

"Once you're sure the techs are under control, do whatever you can to help her."

Luke nodded, got up, straightened his black turtleneck sweater and walked over to the coat rack to get his coat. Normally quiet and self-contained, he seemed more serious than ever. Emily Bradford's murder appeared to weigh heavily on him.

Ed, picking up on Ben's earlier comment about not being able to direct the preliminary investigation, asked his old friend what was going on with his family that he needed to go out of town.

"Ellen flew out last night for Phoenix. Her dad has cancer and is not doing well, and she and her mom think he's only got a few days left," he responded, waving away the server, coffee pot in hand, who came over to the table to see if he wanted a refill.

"That's why Chief and I met so early this morning," interjected Carrie. "He called last night and told me about it and wanted to brief me in person before he left for Arizona."

"Sorry, Ben. What a tough time," remarked Ed.

"It is. When I talked with Ellen earlier this morning she told me her dad's body is starting to shut down. I'd like to go and say goodbye to him and give some support to her and help with the funeral arrangements. Our daughter, Hanna, goes to the University of Arizona and is driving up from Tucson to be with her mother. Neil, our son, is flying in from Purdue, and Ellen's brother and sisters are on their way to Arizona from Cleveland as we speak."

"I promised Annie I wasn't going to take any more consulting jobs until after the holidays, so I probably shouldn't be asking this, but is there anything I can do to help you with the investigation?" Ed asked.

"Yes, as long as it won't cause problems between you and Annie. If I hire you as a criminal consultant, can you work with Carrie? She's got a lot on her plate, especially since she'll have to take my place as chief while I'm away, and I could be gone for a week or more. I'll pay you the hourly rate you've charged in the past when you've helped us with other cases."

Ed, looking thoughtful, nodded. Born and raised in Lighthouse Cove, he had attended the University of Syracuse as an undergraduate, majoring in forensic science, which is where he'd met Annie, a native of Binghamton, who was majoring in social work. They married after graduation, he joined the Navy, attended officers' training school, and after retiring as a rear admiral with the SEALs enrolled at the Rochester Institute of Technology where he obtained a Master's degree in criminal justice. He'd run a violent crimes unit in Albany before moving to Lighthouse Cove to take over as police chief.

"Yes, but only until Christmas. Hopefully we'll have solved the crime by then. Annie and I are taking our kids and grandkids to Disney World and then on a Caribbean cruise between Christmas and New Year's. We're pretty excited about having our family captive on a boat for several days," he responded, eyes twinkling.

"Good motivation for closing the case," Ben noted. "Can you start right now? You're sure this won't cause a problem between you and Annie?"

"I can, and Annie will be fine. She laughed when I told her last night that I wasn't going to take on any more work until after the holidays."

Ed looked at Carrie. "Carrie, I'll begin by interviewing the board members to see if they have any thoughts about why someone might burglarize the museum or knowledge about Emily's personal life. If you can spare Luke once he's finished at the museum, we can also fingerprint them at the same time. We really don't know if Emily was just in the wrong place at the wrong time, or if her murder was premeditated and made to look like a random act. We'll also need to notify next of kin."

"That works for me, Ed. While you're doing that, I'm going to go to the museum and see if the techs need anything and pull Luke away from the murder scene to help me secure Emily's house," Carrie replied. "If there's even a remote possibility that her murder was premeditated then we'll need to go through her personal things: emails, odd pieces of snail mail, messages on her answering machine or anything else that may give us some clues about her killer. When we're finished, I'll have him track you down so you both can begin to fingerprint the board members. We don't want to leave any stones unturned."

Chapter 7

By 7 p.m. that night the snow had stopped, but the wind still howled through the village, rattling the unfallen leaves on the oak trees and twisting the branches of ancient maples into ghoulish silhouettes of human limbs.

After a long, tense day, Ed and Annie, with Gretchen curled up in a little ball beside her, sat on oversized cocoa-colored leather chairs in their living room. Their legs stretched out on a huge matching ottoman, they chatted as they sipped glasses of Cabernet Franc purchased from a nearby Finger Lakes winery and nibbled on vegetable chips and a warm caramelized Vidalia onion dip that Annie had quickly assembled after leaving the museum that afternoon. They could hear the sea as it pitched its angry roar upwards toward the house and the waves as they slapped against the beach below them.

Built for a ship's captain in the mid-1800s, with a rooftop widow's walk that was accessed by a spiral staircase leading up from the attic, the rambling cedar shingled home's wide wrap-around porch faced the lake, with a detached two-bay garage, built in the 1960s to resemble a carriage house, located street side. Inside, the home featured 10-foot ceilings, a claw-foot tub in the main bathroom, original stained Douglas Fir floors, chestnut trim and doors, a large dining room, study, butler's pantry, capacious eat-in kitchen, several bedrooms, and in the living room, built in bookcases flanking the fireplace, which now burned with a crackling fire.

Ed asked Annie if she'd found anything missing at the museum.

"I don't think so but won't know for sure until I'm able to check the inventory list in my computer at the museum. I had emailed myself a copy so that I'd have one here, but since Emily kept it current, the last time I did it was in April. It's not really up to date," Annie responded.

"Once the techs are finished I'll be able to call a couple of docents to help me put things back where they belong and will be able to print out the most recent list, but Luke said I'll need to wait a while before doing that. I'm hoping nothing of value has been taken."

She smiled and changed the subject. "Inveterate match maker that I am, I wish we knew someone we could fix Luke up with. I want everybody to be as happy as we are, and he seems bright and is very attractive."

Ed laughed. "I expect every available young woman in the village has recognized that. He was at our meeting at the bistro this morning, and you should have seen Terri. She was so sweet she was practically turning into a lump of sugar before our eyes."

Annie grinned. "No surprise there. Terri has been seeking a suitable mate for years, and this village doesn't have an abundance of men who would meet her standards. Did he express any interest in her?"

"Not at all. But he'd been up most of the night and had just started investigating a horrible murder. I don't think expanding his social life was on his agenda."

Annie nodded and continued, "Anyway, while I was looking to see if anything was missing at the museum, we talked a little. He wasn't very talkative, probably because he was so focused on the task at hand, but I managed to pry out of him that he's 33, from Connecticut, doesn't have family here, and is a former Navy SEAL."

Getting up from his chair to put a few more logs in the fire, Ed turned to Annie and said, "Ben gave me his background at our meeting this morning, and it appears we might have some things in common. Why don't you invite him over for dinner once things settle down? Since he doesn't have any family in the area he might appreciate a home-cooked meal."

"I was thinking the same thing. I'll talk with him about some dates he might be available," Annie promised.

Ed changed the subject. "Anyway, I'm glad nothing seems to be missing at the museum. I know you've got a lot of valuable historical pieces there."

"Fortunately, nothing was broken, although putting everything back in its place is going to be a real challenge." She sighed. "I just can't shake the image of Emily being killed. It's horrible and so sad."

After pausing for a few seconds, she continued, "While I don't think anything was taken, Ed, I did find something on the floor behind Emily's desk I'd never seen before."

"Something you think might be pertinent to the case?"

"I'm not sure. The back of one of my earrings fell off, so I squatted down to see if I could find it. I couldn't see very well so I was running my hands along the edge of the area rug when I felt something partially hidden under it."

"What was it?"

"A 14-carat gold ship's anchor pendant with a trident down the center of the front. It was monogrammed with our initials. We monogram all our fine jewelry, but this was a little different than some of the others and a bit larger. It wasn't in a box or plastic sleeve, so the logical explanation is that Emily had purchased it but hadn't packaged it yet. I remember that's one of the tasks she had planned to do this week. There was no chain with it which makes sense, since we sell those separately. I'm assuming it could have fallen off her desk during her altercation with the murderer."

"Yet you sound doubtful that it's something she purchased for the gift shop. Did you show it to Luke?"

"I did. For some reason, my instincts are telling me it could be related to Emily's murder. When I handed it to him, he seemed very surprised. But then he said that the techs probably missed it during their first go around the building but probably would have found it when they went through it again. He decided that just in case it is evidence, he'd get it to Carrie to be analyzed. He had already taken his gloves off, but he said he'd let Carrie know that both our prints could be on it. Even if it's too small for prints to show up, he said there could be hair or smudges from blood."

"Luke did the right thing by taking it to Carrie, but she didn't say anything to me about it. Maybe you're first assumption that Emily had purchased but had not had time to package it is correct, despite your uneasiness. Everyone's a bit on edge right now."

"Did you find out anything when you interviewed the board members?" asked Annie.

"Everyone's in shock, especially Charles. They all respected Emily, but from what I could gather she was very private about her personal life, so no one, other than Suzanne, who was a good friend, knew that much about her.

"Anyway," Ed continued, "Suzanne told me there's an estranged husband—an art dealer and gallery owner—living in Rochester. His name is Jonathan, and the gallery is located on Park Street. Emily told her the split was amicable, and that the divorce is not yet final.

"She also told me Emily's parents are dead and she was unaware of any siblings, so the husband may be the only surviving relative. The *Rochester Democrat and Chronicle* plus a couple of TV stations picked up on the story from the police logs and wanted to run with it tonight, but Carrie got them to agree to not name the victim, pending notification to the family. I plan to go see him tomorrow morning."

"That's interesting. I assumed she was already divorced. By the way, did you know Emily's maiden name was Parisi?"

"Parisi? Why is that name familiar to me?" Ed squinted, trying to remember, as he brought the glass of wine up to his lips and took a sip. Then his eyes opened wide in recognition as he glanced down at his glass. "Is Emily related to the Parisi family who owns the winery on Cayuga Lake where this wine was made?"

Annie nodded. "The very same. The vintners were her parents, and she's an heiress. Her parents are, as Suzanne told you, dead, but they didn't die of natural causes. It's a very sad story.

"Several years ago, before Emily moved here, there was a tragic accident on Rt. 90. Emily's parents were driving back from their summer home in Vermont and were hit by a drunk driver. Emily's mom was killed instantly, and her dad was severely injured. He never recovered emotionally or physically and died some months later. It made all the papers."

"Now that you mention it, I do remember reading about that. How devastating that must have been for Emily."

"There's more to this story, Ed. Some months before the accident, the family was approached by Marchal Lacroix Vineyards, a French winemaker that wanted to acquire a winery in the States. Parisi Vineyards, as you may know, has been featured in *Wine Spectator, Food and Wine,* and *The New York Times* weekend magazine, and they'd won multiple awards for their Dry Riesling and Cabernet Franc. The Parisis sold out to Lacroix, made millions and retired. And then, of course, shortly after that they were killed."

"How do you know about this?" Ed asked.

"Emily asked to meet privately with me about six months ago. She told me about her family history and that she wanted to create an endowment fund for the museum, but she wanted to do it anonymously. It was a significant amount of money. The interest alone would have paid for part of my salary and the upkeep on the building in perpetuity. She obviously had to take me into her confidence."

"How much money was she talking about?"

Annie sighed. "Half a million dollars. We were working out the details through her attorneys, but I was sworn to secrecy. I couldn't even tell other members of the board. Or you."

Ed stared at Annie in disbelief. "The museum is going to receive a $500,000 endowment, and you managed to keep it a secret from me? How could you not tell me? We tell each other everything."

"Believe me, Ed, it was really hard. But a promise is a promise. I was almost beside myself when Emily told me what she wanted to do, but I just couldn't betray a confidence. Now of course it may never happen, but in the long run we are no worse off than we were before, and a lovely woman is dead. It's so sad."

"So, there's a possibility that the husband could inherit a huge sum of money," Ed mused. "It would be nice to know what his financial situation is. If he has money problems, it may be we now have our first person of interest."

Chapter 8

The snow began falling again at around 3:00 the next morning, and by the time the DeCleryks were up and moving at 7:00 a.m. there were several more inches on the ground. Ed told Annie that despite the storm he planned to go into Rochester later that morning to talk with Jonathan Bradford.

"Aren't you going to call before you go? It's a long drive into Rochester. What if he's not there?" asked Annie.

"I called yesterday and spoke with his receptionist, pretending to be a collector. I told her I was interested in looking at some sculpture to purchase and wanted to know if the owner would be at the studio today. She said he was out of town for a meeting, but he'd be back this morning. I'll call around 9:00 just to make sure the gallery isn't closed because of the snow. If it is, then I'll see if I can track him down another way."

"Why don't you consider packing an overnight bag? This weather is crazy, and if it keeps on snowing you may have trouble getting home tonight."

"Annie, you know as well as I do that our SUV will get me into Rochester and back here without any problems."

"I do, but I'd still feel better if you would take along a change of clothes, just in case. You never know where your interview with Jonathan Bradford will lead you, and you might be in the city longer than you expect. Once it gets dark, even with diligent snow removal efforts on the highways, the back roads to Lighthouse Cove could be very icy."

Ed sighed. "Point well taken. I'll pack a bag because I don't want you to worry, but expect me home by dinnertime. I'll call if that changes. What are you planning to do today?"

"I thought I'd go into the basement of the museum to look through some of the boxes that are stored there that I haven't had time to go through since taking this job. Just after Donna resigned to go back to England and right before I started, she told me about them and said they might contain archived materials, and I use the term 'archived' loosely. She never had time to go through them either, and for all I know they could be filled with paper goods left over from cookouts and picnics or crafts' materials from summer camp. Since I can't do much of anything else right now, I figured I could at least start that project."

"It seems a bit premature for you to go there today, Annie. The building is still a crime scene, and as Luke told you, the techs will probably search the building one last time just to make sure they didn't miss anything. That's why Luke didn't want you to start putting things away just yet. I'm also concerned about you being by yourself. There's always the possibility the intruder could return at some point to search for whatever it was he was after, and I want you to be safe."

"Ed, whoever did this isn't going to come back to the site in broad daylight," argued Annie impatiently. "I can't imagine the techs will find any additional fingerprints and hair samples that haven't already been collected,"

Ed responded, "Why don't you check with Carrie first to make sure she's okay with your being there today, and if she is, ask her if she'd let Luke come with you. I'll feel better knowing you're safe, and Luke can let you know if he and the techs are finished."

"Ed, I mentioned to Luke that I might want to go into the basement today, and he didn't seem to have a problem with it."

"Did he actually *tell* you he had no problem with your being there? That's hard for me to believe."

"Well, not exactly. He kind of grunted, and in fairness he did seem a bit preoccupied and probably really wasn't listening all that carefully to what I said. Still, I can't imagine it would be a problem. I can wear gloves if necessary, so I don't contaminate anything with my fingerprints."

"Annie, those boxes could be heavy, and the basement is probably cold and dirty, but there's no way you'll be cleared to look at them in your office just yet. If Carrie agrees that you can go into the building today maybe Luke could help you bring them back here where you can work at your leisure without my worrying about you."

Annie sighed. "Fine. I'll call Carrie, but just because you're asking. Hopefully she'll agree and let Luke come with me. Be safe, and call me when you can."

Chapter 9

The drive into downtown Rochester across Irondequoit Bay was easier than Ed expected. The snow was still falling, but department of transportation workers driving oversized snow removal trucks were out in numbers, keeping the roads mostly clear.

Ed found a parking spot in front of Gallery 21, and at just a few minutes after 10 a.m., walked up four steps to the entrance of the red brick Federal-style building that stood hip-to-hip with others on the tree-lined street. A large black door with a brass lion's head knocker was bordered on either side by a glass and black iron coach lamp, and shiny black shutters flanked the two mullioned windows located to the right of the front door and the four identical windows on the second story.

Inside the gallery, glossy black walls with white trim and polished pickled oak hardwood floors created a dramatic framework for the artwork, which consisted of several pieces of metal sculpture displayed on clear acrylic pedestals, plus black and white photos and colorful abstracts, illuminated from above by subdued recessed lighting.

A stunning, slender, tall young woman with arresting emerald green cat's eyes and wavy flame-colored hair cascading down to her waist rose from a clear acrylic chair that sat behind an eight-foot rectangular stainless-steel table. She was dressed head to toe in black: mini-dress, tights, knee-high boots and large dangling enameled hoop earrings.

"Hi, may I help you?" she asked. "My name is Sophie."

Ed, who was dressed in business attire, replied, "Sophie, my name is Ed DeCleryk. I called yesterday about wanting to meet with Jonathan Bradford today. Is he available?"

"I remember your call, Mr. DeCleryk," she replied, with a warm, wide smile. "He's on his way. He was in Buffalo when the storm hit and decided to spend the night. I'm glad he did because I was very concerned about his safety," she said with warmth and caring in her voice.

"He phoned a little while ago and told me some of the main highways weren't able to be cleared until this morning, so he got a later start back than he expected.

"If you'd care to wait, he should be here within the next several minutes. Can I offer you some coffee or tea? I also have some wonderful croissants and muffins from the bakery next door. They're still warm."

"No, thanks. I'll just wander around and look at the sculpture until he gets here."

"There are three more rooms behind this one. Let me know if you have any questions or if any of the pieces interest you, and I'll be sure to let Jon know you're here when he arrives."

About ten minutes later, a slim-hipped, broad-shouldered man just over six-feet tall, wearing gray flannel slacks, a black mock-turtleneck sweater, black worsted wool sports coat and shiny black tasseled leather loafers, ambled through the entrance from the front exhibit space.

Smiling with his hand extended, he said, "Good morning, Mr. DeCleryk. I just got here, and Sophie told me you wanted to see me. I'm Jon Bradford. How may I help you?"

The handsome gallery owner appeared to be his mid-to-late 40s, had short, shiny black hair combed back away from his forehead, aquamarine-colored eyes fringed with long, dark lashes and a well-tended dark stubble covering his sculpted, finely-boned face. Despite his sophisticated appearance, his smile was warm and genuine, and his eyes were gentle.

"Good morning, Mr. Bradford. Is there somewhere we can speak privately?"

"Sophie said you were interested in purchasing some sculpture. Why do we need to speak privately?"

"Please indulge me," Ed said. "I'd prefer discussing business somewhere other than this lobby."

Jon glanced at Sophie with a quizzical look and politely said, "Of course. My office is in the back. Please come this way."

On their way through the gallery spaces Ed put a hand on Jon's shoulder and stopped walking. "I'm so sorry for the subterfuge, but I'm not a collector," he said quietly. "I'm the retired police chief from Lighthouse Cove and want to talk with you about a case I've been hired by the current chief to work on as a criminal consultant. It's personal, and I didn't want to tell Sophie about the reason for my call." Ed pulled out his identification and handed it to Jon.

Jon glanced at Ed's ID card. "Emily, my wife, lives in Lighthouse Cove." He paused. "Oh, my God. Has something happened to her?"

Ed responded, "If you don't mind, let's go into your office and sit down."

The office decor complemented the gallery. The walls in this space were a pale silvery gray with dove gray trim, and a 1960s black glass Parsons table served as Jonathan's desk. Bucket-shaped chairs upholstered in ivory suede, a chandelier with a multitude of glass prisms, and a cream and gray chevron patterned rug covering most of the polished concrete floor, created a dramatic appearance. An immense, overgrown fern in a large concrete urn sat in a corner, a recessed grow-light shining down on it from the ceiling.

Jon Bradford's eyes welled up with tears when Ed informed him about Emily's death. He seemed genuinely shocked and distressed, but Ed had enough experience as an investigator to know that charming men could also be sociopaths and as such, convincing actors.

When he realized part of Ed's mission was to question him about his whereabouts on the night of Emily's death, Jon volunteered that he would have been the last person who wanted Emily dead.

"I learned the two of you had separated." Jon nodded. "Why?" Ed asked.

Jon sighed, his voice catching as he responded, "It's a long story. Emily had had some real tragedy in her life. Her parents had been killed by a drunken driver on Rt. 90, and as an only child she had no one, other than me, to lean on."

Ed responded, "That's very sad and must have been terribly difficult for her."

"It was, and it put a strain on our marriage, although we'd been having some problems before that. My long hours and frequent business trips, her devotion to her students that consumed so much of her time, all of it took precedence over our relationship. I suppose her parents' death took her over the edge. She became increasingly more withdrawn at home."

Jon admitted that Emily's emotional distance bothered him, but he had no idea what was really going on until she confessed she had recently ended an affair with a Xerox executive named Eric Sewall, a student in one of the creative writing classes she'd taught a couple of nights a week for older adult learners. She told Jon that when she'd met Eric he was separated from his wife. He'd been kind and exceptionally attentive, which, given her vulnerability at the time, was very seductive.

Eric was also needy and emotionally unstable. A few months after the affair started, he told Emily he planned to get a divorce and began pressuring her to divorce Jon and marry him. She realized she was not in love with him and still loved Jon, so broke things off. Obsessed and desperate, he started stalking her, showing up outside her classroom, waiting for her in the parking lot near the building where she taught, sending flowers to her at her office, texting her at all hours of the day and night.

"I was terribly angry and very upset with Emily but also concerned about her safety and suggested she go to the police about the stalking," Jon said. "She believed, and at the time I thought it was reasonable, that if she ignored Eric he would eventually go away."

"She said she loved me and hoped we could work on saving our marriage. I still loved her and didn't want to see an end to years of a happy relationship so I forgave her, but when I suggested we get counseling she refused, saying that she simply didn't have the energy for it. Then it seemed that all we did was argue, and after several tense months, we separated, and she moved into a small studio apartment near the campus. Both of us hoped the separation was temporary and that after some cooling off time we would eventually get back together."

Ed sat silently while Jon put his hands over his eyes and wept. After several minutes he stopped, took a couple of shaky breaths and apologized.

"Jon, you've just received horrible news. No need to apologize."

Jon shook his head. "I'll be all right. I just need a little time to pull myself together."

After a couple of minutes, he took another deep breath and continued, "Emily and I kept in touch, and I found out that ignoring Eric hadn't worked and the stalking had escalated. She called and begged him to leave her alone, reiterating that she was no longer interested in continuing their relationship. He must have been really desperate to get her back, because he then threatened to go to her department head with details about the affair." Jon took a breath and shook his head.

"How did Emily respond to the threat?" Ed asked.

"Emily didn't want scandal tied to her name, or to mine," Jon said. "She was respected and well-liked. She finally went to the police, took out a PFA against Eric and decided to take an early retirement and move to Lighthouse Cove. The overt stalking stopped after the PFA, but we have no idea if he really went away. Maybe you should be looking at him as a suspect."

Ed, ignoring Jon's last remark, changed the subject. "I recently learned Emily was an heiress. She obviously worked because she enjoyed having a career and not because she needed money. It must have been difficult for her to decide to retire."

"That's true. She didn't need the money. She worked because she loved what she was doing, but her emotional state was so fragile that she couldn't concentrate on her job. She retired because she felt as though she had no other options. I believed this would have blown over and tried to get her to reconsider, but she was resolute. We both had always loved Lighthouse Cove and had talked about buying a house there, and she decided that now was the time for her to do that. We still keep in touch," Jon said, using the present tense, "I've never stopped loving her."

Ed was beginning to believe that Jon Bradford had nothing to do with Emily's murder, and that he might have a point about the ex-lover as a suspect. Still, he had to take the next step in the interview.

"Sophie said you were in Buffalo last night," he said, changing the subject. "Please give me the details about the trip."

"I know you have to ask about my whereabouts. I have no problem with that. I went to meet with an up-and-coming glass sculptor to see her work. I can give you her name and contact information. While she's not yet in the same stratosphere as Dale Chihuly, she has incredible promise, and I wanted to talk with her about exhibiting here at Gallery 21.

"I got on the thruway at about 6:45 a.m. and planned to come back last night, but the storm you got here yesterday morning didn't get to Buffalo until late afternoon. We got more snow than you did, and visibility was almost zero, so to play it safe I got a room downtown at the Hyatt, had dinner in the hotel's restaurant, and was in bed and asleep by about 11 p.m."

"Can you provide me with proof you made the trip to Buffalo yesterday?"

"Yes, I can. I have EZ Pass and will give you my account number and make and model of my car, and you can check with NYDOT. I also have receipts from the hotel and meals—I took the sculptor out to lunch—and from the gas station where I filled up. I'll be happy to show them to you," he volunteered.

Jon gave Ed the sculptor's name and phone number, his EZ pass account and license plate numbers and produced the receipts from his briefcase. Ed planned to follow-up, but Jon's alibi seemed credible and the man seemed genuinely grief-stricken over Emily's death. But was his alibi too well-constructed? He wondered if Jon, furious at her infidelity, could have hired someone to murder Emily while he was on his business trip and made it look like she was killed as the result of the museum burglary.

"One more question, please. Is your gallery profitable? Just the maintenance on a building like this, plus utilities, insurance and the need for an advanced security system, must cost a bundle."

Jon shook his head. "I know what you're inferring. The gallery's doing fine, but even if it weren't, I wouldn't need Emily's money to help with any shortfalls. Just so you know, I have plenty of my own from a very large trust fund. My ancestors came over to this country on the Mayflower, and most of my family still lives in Boston. They own several breweries and have some real estate holdings on Cape Cod. You're probably familiar with some of our beers and ales."

"Bradford Brewing Company is your family's business?" Jon nodded. "Of course, I know it. Every restaurant, bar, package store and supermarket in this area carries a selection of your products."

Ed paused before continuing, "So, what brought you to Rochester to run a gallery? From what you've just told me, you wouldn't have to work if you didn't want to."

"That's true, but the thought never crossed my mind to not have a career. I've always loved art, particularly sculpture, and was fortunate to have parents who encouraged me and my two brothers to follow our dreams. Emily and I moved here from Boston after I got my master of fine arts degree and she got her doctorate in creative writing and was offered the position at the university. Rochester has such a vibrant arts' scene that it was the perfect place for me to open a gallery."

"You're fortunate your parents didn't pressure you into staying in the business."

"Yes, I am. My brother Ethan chose to be involved in the family business and is now the chairman of the brewery corporation, but my brother Ted's an oncology doctor, living in Chicago."

"Can you think of anyone who could have benefited financially from Emily's death?"

"No. Neither of us was each other's beneficiary, we didn't need to be. After she became an heiress, Emily created a foundation that's run by a law firm headed by an old family friend. She was setting up a large endowment for the museum in Lighthouse Cove, and the foundation's other donations go to support the arts, human services and education. She has no living blood relatives, and other than the museum, there were no caveats that her money would go to any specific organization after her death, as far as I'm aware."

"What about Sophie? Knowing you and Emily were talking reconciliation, could she have been jealous enough to want her out of the way?"

"Sophie? You think Sophie and I are involved?" Jon barked out a laugh. "I haven't even dated since Emily and I separated. I just told you we had hoped to get back together, and I certainly wouldn't muddy the waters by seeing someone else. I'm flattered you think such a beautiful young woman would be interested in me, but nothing could be farther from the truth."

"She seems inordinately fond of you."

"She is, as I am of her. Sophie is my niece, the oldest daughter of my brother Ted and his wife, Claire. She graduated in the spring from the Eastman School of Music and stayed on in Rochester to perform with a chamber music group as its violinist, along with her boyfriend, Jason, who plays the cello.

"Most of their rehearsals and performances are in the evening, so when my previous receptionist and her husband, who's an architect, moved to Ottawa a couple of months ago so he could take a job there, I asked Sophie if she wanted to work for me. She agreed, but made sure I understood there might be times she would be unavailable if asked to perform or rehearse during the day. She loved Emily. They met for lunch every Wednesday and were, in fact, somewhat kindred spirits. She'll be devastated to hear about her death."

Ed left the gallery after Jon called Sophie into his office to tell her about Emily. She sobbed, doubled over with grief, while Jon, tears running down his cheeks, held her. Promising not only to find her killer but to call as soon as Emily's body could be released so funeral arrangements could be made, Ed gave Jon his card which contained his email address and cell phone number and asked them to contact him if they could think of anything at all that might help him find Emily's murderer.

He'd check his alibi, but he believed Jon had been truthful. The next step would be to seek out the former lover. A PFA could have infuriated him, and if he were emotionally unstable the stalking may have continued without Emily's knowledge.

Chapter 10

Ed called the corporate headquarters for Xerox, which was less than half an hour's drive from downtown Rochester, hoping to speak with Eric Sewall. A receptionist answered. When he asked to be connected to Sewall's office, she put him on hold and then after a few seconds informed Ed that he was not listed in the company directory.

"Do you know where he's working now?"

"Sir, I don't have that information," the receptionist replied politely. "I don't even know if he worked here, either. I've only been here for three weeks. I can connect you to the Human Resources Department, maybe they can help you. Please hold."

Ed waited for about a minute when another woman, who identified herself as Denise, finally answered. When he asked about Sewall, she answered politely that she couldn't give any information about employees or former employees over the phone and that he would need to speak directly with the human resources director, Phillip Miller.

"Could you transfer me to his extension, please?" He waited a few seconds, and then Denise came back on the line informing him that Miller was at a meeting but that he had an opening at 1:30 if Ed wanted to meet with him then. Disappointed he wouldn't be able to talk directly with Sewall, Ed thanked her and told her he'd see Mr. Miller at the appointed time. Annie may have been right. The day was going to be a long one.

Having more time on his hands than he expected and by now a bit hungry, Ed decided to take an early lunch and walked a half block down the street from the gallery to a pub located next to a quaint shop he thought Annie might like, its display windows featuring an eclectic array of gifts, greeting cards, boutique clothing and packaged gourmet mixes.

Sitting at the bar, he ordered a turkey burger with lettuce and tomato on a whole grain bun, sweet potato fries and an iced tea. On impulse, he decided to see if he could talk with the head of Emily's department at the university before going on to Xerox. Maybe that person would have some additional insights about Emily and her former lover, Eric Sewall.

He called the university switchboard and was connected directly to Dr. Diane Dawson, the chairperson of the writing department, who happened to be in her office. Shocked when he informed her about Emily's death, Dr. Dawson agreed to meet with Ed at 12:30. He gobbled down the rest of his sandwich, motioned for the bill, and after paying it and leaving a generous tip, walked to his car and headed to the university.

Chapter 11

While Ed was in Rochester, Luke and Carrie, who had obtained a key from Suzanne Gordon, drove to Emily's house to continue the investigation they had started the day before. Carrie told Luke Annie had called her requesting permission to go into the museum basement to get some boxes to bring home and that she'd said Luke had given his approval yesterday.

Luke responded that he'd been so preoccupied with the details surrounding the investigation that he didn't remember the conversation, which didn't surprise Carrie, given the events of the past couple of days and his lack of sleep. She agreed he could help Annie after they finished their work there.

They had just pulled into the driveway when a tech from the crime lab called and reported that while there were plenty of prints found at the museum, they either belonged to board members or staff or couldn't be identified.

Surrounded on three sides by water, the house sat at the end of a mile-long peninsula that jutted into Silver Bay at the mouth of the lake. While within walking distance of the small business district, the site had afforded Emily quite a bit of privacy during the off-season since most of her neighbors were professionals who came from the cities during summer months or retirees who left to spend their winters in warmer climates.

There was no security system; most residents didn't have one, as there was little crime in Lighthouse Cove.

Being within proximity of Canada and on a major international waterway, the village enjoyed the protection of local and state police, the Coast Guard and Homeland Security.

Donning disposable paper coveralls, booties and plastic gloves, the two investigators entered the house with fingerprinting equipment and cases that would be the repository for collected hair, clothing and blood samples to send to the crime lab in Rochester for evaluation. The systematic search began in the foyer, then into the living room and throughout the rest of the house.

Carrie was struck by the simplicity of the décor, with colors that blended in with the natural outdoor surroundings, mimicking the sea, sand, beach grasses and sky, and radiating light from the many windows facing the water. Books of all sizes and topics lined shelves in every room. In the kitchen, gleaming copper pots and pans hung on a rack above a large cherry island with a black granite top sparkling with gold, green and rust-colored chips. Cherry cabinets with mullioned glass doors contained crystal wine and beverage glasses and simple white dinnerware, and lower drawers revealed tableware and tidy piles of colorful linens. An array of cookbooks, shelved in order of subject matter, lined a built-in case on one wall.

Nothing seemed out of order in the living room, dining room, bathrooms or guest bedrooms, and Carrie began to believe Emily had been in the wrong place at the wrong time and her murder was a random, and not premeditated, act. But they hadn't yet combed the kitchen, her bedroom or study for evidence, saving those rooms for last since they were most likely the spaces where Emily had spent the most personal time.

Emily's computer, located in her study, had been turned on and was not password protected, so Carrie had no trouble accessing her files. She perused the Word documents first. Emily had been working on a book of poetry, lovely old-fashioned sonnets about love and loss, but there was nothing suspicious in that file or any of the others. She then started looking through her emails and found a string of them that caused her breath to catch. She called Luke into the room and after he read the emails and agreed with her that they were concerning, she copied and pasted them into a flash drive she carried with her on her key chain and forwarded them to herself via email.

Chapter 12

Ed pulled into the parking lot in front of the Liberal Arts building at the university at just a few minutes before 12:30. The snow had stopped, but the parking lot was slick, so he carefully made his way to the entrance of the building, arriving just a few minutes late. The gray-haired department head, dressed in a black wool pants suit with a black, green and cream-colored scarf wrapped around her neck and black suede pumps, greeted him in the lobby of the building and escorted him back to her office.

She was dismayed at the news of Emily's death, her warm brown eyes glittering with tears. She told Ed that Emily had been not only a fine teacher but also a lovely, kind person. Her students had adored her, and many had gone on to enjoy successful careers as writers, editors and teachers. Ed asked the dean if she'd known about Emily's affair with Eric Sewall.

She responded that she'd known about the affair, but not until Eric Sewall started stalking Emily and she'd confided in her, fearing the situation would become public.

"I'm not naïve, Mr. DeCleryk. Affairs between students and professors are more commonplace than you might think even though we frown on them, and in Emily's case, with a marriage on the rocks and the tragic death of her parents, it wasn't surprising. She was vulnerable, and despite the unwritten policy here, what she did was her business as long as it didn't negatively affect the university or her ability to teach."

"Why did she leave? I know she was horribly stressed, but quitting her job seems somewhat of an overreaction."

"She was ashamed of her behavior and concerned about her reputation and the impact of her actions on her husband and here at the university," replied Dr. Dawson. "This would have blown over for Emily, but she thought otherwise."

"It sounds like you tried to convince her to stay. Did she think she had no other options?"

"Her emotional state at the time wasn't good to begin with because of everything going on in her life. I suggested she take a leave of absence, get some professional help and then come back, but she thought she needed a complete change, said she was burned out, and resigned. We kept in touch, and I offered more than once to reinstate her if she changed her mind and wanted to teach here again."

"Is there anyone here on campus who you believe might have wanted her dead?" asked Ed.

Dr. Dawson sighed and shook her head. "I can't think of a soul. I just can't imagine any of her colleagues, students or even former students who would have that much animosity towards her. There must be other suspects. Eric Sewall should be on your list. I learned from Emily that he was separated from his wife. Did the separation have anything to do with their affair? Could his wife be a suspect? While Jon Bradford strikes me as a decent man, could he have done it? What about someone in Lighthouse Cove?"

Ed responded, "Our investigation is just beginning, but we're exploring every possible avenue. Her murder could have been a random act, the result of a burglary gone badly, or very possibly, someone she knew. We just don't know yet."

"I wish there was more I could do, Chief DeCleryk. I'm betting on Sewall."

"I promise you we'll find whoever killed Emily and make sure that person is put away for life," he said.

Chapter 13

Leaving the building, Ed walked carefully to his car. The snow had started falling again, so he retrieved his snow brush from the rear of the SUV, dusted off the windshield and windows and got into the vehicle, turning his defroster to "high". He'd turned off his cell phone before his meeting with Diane Dawson, and turning it back on, noticed a text from Carrie. "Call me. I think I found something!"

He needed to get to his next interview with the human resources director at Xerox, and cautious about the weather, wanted to give himself some extra time. He texted Carrie back, "Heading to meet with HR Dir. @ Xerox. Will call you ASAP."

During his drive to Xerox, Ed thought it more and more plausible that Eric Sewall, unstable and desperate, might have murdered Emily because she'd rejected him. He wondered if Eric could have driven to Lighthouse Cove sometime before dawn, which is why Luke wouldn't have noticed any suspicious cars earlier in the evening, parked his car in a parking lot in the business district near her home or on one of the side streets, followed her to the museum the next morning and in a rage killed her, then trashed the building to make it look like a burglary.

When Ed arrived at Xerox, the receptionist ushered him into Phillip Miller's office where the director was waiting to speak with him. The slender, medium height, gray-haired man was dressed in a subtle window-pane checked gray worsted wool suit, crisply starched white shirt, and blue and yellow striped tie.

Rising gracefully from behind his desk to shake hands with Ed, he motioned him into a chair before sitting back down. He asked—coolness in his voice— why Ed wanted to know if Eric Sewall worked there.

Taking his credentials out of his jacket pocket and handing them to Miller, Ed informed him that he was a consultant with the police department at Lighthouse Cove and that he was doing some checking on the man for reasons he couldn't divulge. He decided he didn't want Sewall's credibility to be damaged if, in fact, he turned out to be another unproductive lead.

Miller verified that Sewall, a mechanical engineer, had worked as the head of the outsourcing division for one of their product lines, but didn't offer any additional information about him other than to say that he was no longer employed there, even when Ed pressed him about where he'd gone.

"All I'm required to do by law, Mr. DeCleryk, is verify that Eric did work here at one time," Miller responded sternly.

Ed decided to be more forthcoming and told Miller he had been hesitant to tell him the real reason for his visit because of the sensitive nature of the inquiry but that he was investigating a murder that had taken place the previous day in Lighthouse Cove. Eric Sewall's name had come up as a possible person of interest.

"If you know where he is, Mr. Miller, I'd really appreciate your telling me, so I can talk with him and then hopefully rule him out as a suspect."

"You say the murder occurred yesterday?"

Ed nodded.

"Then Eric Sewall couldn't possibly have been involved," Miller stated with conviction.

"How could you know that?"

"I know it because Eric's dead. Has been for several months."

Stunned, but wondering if there might be more information that Miller was withholding, Ed asked if Eric's death had been the result of foul play.

"You mean was he murdered? Of course not, why would you think that?"

"He had an affair with the woman who was murdered last night. I'm wondering if there could be a connection between their deaths," Ed responded, now thinking that perhaps Sewall's wife might be involved.

"I can't imagine there would be. Eric died of natural causes."

"Still, I'd appreciate your cooperating with me, Mr. Miller. If their deaths weren't related, do you think he could have arranged to have her killed before he died? You obviously knew him and have no need to protect him now."

Miller grimaced. "I'll answer your questions, but I'm very uncomfortable doing so. Yes, I knew Eric well. He was my close friend as well as a co-worker. What I'll tell you is that he was a family man, doted on his kids, and despite a rocky marriage, really tried to make a go of it. Sherry Sewall isn't the warmest person in the world, and staying married to her was a challenge. They separated a few years ago because she believed he was cheating on her with a co-worker, which was absolutely not true."

"Do you know who she thought he was involved with?" asked Ed.

"Yes. Eileen Rooney was another division head who had been here about ten years before Eric came to Xerox, and she mentored him. She's quite attractive but also happily married, and although there was chemistry between them, their relationship was completely platonic and professional. Sherry had met Eileen and her husband numerous times at company events, picked up on the chemistry and was suspicious that something more was going on.

"Eileen was relocating to North Carolina with her husband, a banker who had obtained a position there, and as a gesture of appreciation before she left, Eric took her out for lunch at a very expensive restaurant here in Rochester. He didn't say anything to Sherry about it because it was during work hours, and he knew how she'd react."

The human resources director told Ed that Eric later confided in him that without thinking, he'd left the receipt from the restaurant in the pocket of his suit coat and Sherry found it when she went through his pockets before taking the coat to the dry cleaner. She confronted him after noticing the luncheon was for two. He could have lied and said his meeting was with a male co-worker but instead admitted the truth and confessed that he hadn't said anything to her because she was so mistrusting. They had a huge argument, she accused him of infidelity and asked him to move out. Desperate to save his marriage because of his kids, Eric told Eileen what happened, and she called Sherry, but Sherry wouldn't speak with her.

"Eric moved out, got an apartment near the University of Rochester and tried to get on with his life, still hoping for reconciliation because he loved his children and didn't want them to suffer the pain of a divorce.

"Then after a time, he seemed at peace and appeared to be content, even happy. Maybe he decided that if his wife was so certain he'd been unfaithful that he had no reason to continue to be loyal to her, and that's when he became involved with your victim," Miller reflected.

"What happened next?" Ed asked.

"About two years ago, he came to me and asked for a transfer. He said there was no hope for his marriage and that he had some personal things going on in his life and needed a change in scenery. He seemed depressed. It must have been when his affair with your victim ended."

Miller continued, "We have offices in Harrisburg, Pennsylvania, and our CEO agreed he could still maintain his current position and work from there as long as he understood he'd have to make regular trips up here for meetings. He agreed and shortly after relocated, but sadly about nine months ago he was diagnosed with stage four pancreatic cancer and died three months later. Eric may have been misguided, maybe even a bit desperate, but I knew him well and he never would have killed anyone. He was a gentle man."

"Is his ex-wife still in the area?" asked Ed, remembering what Diane Dawson had implied about the possibility of the murderer being an irate wife. "I'd like to speak with her." He knew it was a long shot, especially given the chronology of events leading to Eric's death, but decided it wouldn't hurt to pay her a visit on his way back to Lighthouse Cove.

"She is, but if you're thinking that she might have murdered your victim out of some sort of vendetta, I think you're barking up the wrong tree," Miller stated with conviction. "She's prim and proper and somewhat paranoid, but even if she knew about the affair, my sense is she's too devoted a mother to commit a murder and deprive her children of both their parents, should she get caught."

"I can obtain a subpoena to get that information, Mr. Miller. Instead, why don't you voluntarily give it to me? It will make things a lot easier."

Miller, shaking his head in distaste, wrote down Sherry Sewall's address and phone number and gave it to Ed.

Ed thanked him and stood up to leave, but as he got to the door he turned around and faced Miller. "I have one more question. What happened when Eric got sick? Did he stay in Harrisburg or come back to Rochester?"

"The divorce never was finalized, and when Eric was diagnosed he went on disability and moved back up here with his family. It made it easier for Sherry to get his life insurance, his pension and his 401k. Fortunately, she and the children are financially comfortable."

"I still want to speak with her." But as he left Miller's office he thought it seemed more and more likely that the trail to finding Emily's murderer was leading him right back to Lighthouse Cove.

Chapter 14

Ed got into his car and called Sherry Sewall. When she answered the phone, he identified himself and explained he was investigating a murder and that her name had come up as someone who might have information that would be helpful in finding the killer. She was hesitant about agreeing to speak with him; he heard fear and suspicion in her voice.

It took him about twenty minutes to get to Fairport, a quaint village built along the Erie Canal west of Lighthouse Cove. Sherry's sprawling, wood-sided and cobblestoned home, located in the historic district, sat back from the canal. It was framed by a wide yard with large oak and maple trees and although in stages of late autumnal decay, what appeared to be a lush garden.

A sharp-featured, brown-eyed, rail-thin woman of medium height with chin-length graying brown hair parted on one side and pulled back behind her ears answered the door. She was wearing brown woolen slacks, a beige, brown and black tweed woolen turtleneck sweater, and brown flats. She wore no makeup nor any jewelry. She asked Ed for identification and after he showed it, cautiously let him into her foyer.

He offered his condolences and before he could begin questioning her, Sherry Sewall asked sharply, "What's this really about? Why would I know anything about a murder? My children will be home from school soon, so let's get this over with."

Ed responded, "There's a woman in Lighthouse Cove who's been murdered, and I'm wondering if you happened to have known her. Her name is Emily Bradford."

She blinked a few times and then shook her head, looking at him blankly. "That name doesn't sound familiar, should it?"

"She was a professor at the University of Rochester, and just before she retired, your husband took a creative writing course from her. We are questioning some of her students along with others who knew her, just to see if anyone can provide us with information that could help us find her killer," Ed dissembled, not wanting to stir the pot by mentioning the affair.

"How did you get my husband's name?" she asked.

"I got his name from the chairperson of the writing department at the university. I decided to include older adult learners because I believe they might have some better observational skills. I found out from Phillip Miller when I went to Xerox that Eric had died, so while I can't question him, I wondered if Eric had mentioned her to you."

"We were estranged at that time," Sherry replied, visibly more at ease. "We didn't talk much about anything other than the children and our finances. He told me he was taking a course at the university, but I didn't know the details." She then told Ed the same story that Phillip Miller had, about her belief that her husband had had an affair with a co-worker despite his denial, and their subsequent separation.

"My father was a corporate executive, just like Eric," she said, glaring angrily at Ed. "My mother is a nervous, insecure little woman, and I always wondered why. After my father died, she confided in me that he had been consistently unfaithful to her. I never knew why she stayed, economic dependency I guess, like me she was a stay-at-home mom. But there's no way I'd ever go through what she did."

"When I spoke with Phillip Miller at Xerox, he indicated that you and Eric had reconciled before his death," stated Ed, ignoring her tirade.

She answered, "It wasn't exactly a reconciliation. I figured it was only a matter of time until he died, and we both agreed that if we stayed married it would simplify things and it would be easier to settle the estate, so we dropped the divorce proceedings and he came home. It was the least I could do. He is, after all, the father of my children, and I owed him that much, especially since he didn't fight me on a financial settlement."

Ed believed her when she said she didn't know Emily and decided to end the interview. Thanking her and reiterating his condolences, he apologized for taking up her time, and making a quick exit walked to his car to head back to Lighthouse Cove. He felt an odd bit of sympathy for Eric Sewall.

Chapter 15

Back inside his car, Ed dialed Carrie's number. When she answered, he said, "Carrie, it's Ed. Sorry I didn't get back to you sooner, but I was following up on a bunch of leads." He told her about his interviews with Jonathan Bradford, Diane Dawson and Phillip Miller, and of Eric Sewall's death and the interview with his wife.

"Bradford has an alibi, and he was genuinely distressed when he learned about Emily. Sewall's death takes him off the list, and it seems very unlikely he arranged a hit on her before he died. And I'm convinced that his wife, while very unlikeable, knew nothing about Emily or that Sewall had a relationship with her. What's up with you?"

"I found some emails to Emily from Eric Sewall that really concern me. They stopped some months ago, and now I understand why. The last one was an apology for causing Emily distress, and he said he wouldn't be bothering her again. He also said he regretted his actions, that he'd been very needy when he met her, and he hoped she would have a good life. But there's no indication he told her he was dying."

"Interesting. I wonder why Jon Bradford didn't say anything about the last email."

"Maybe Emily never mentioned it to him."

"He knew about Sewall, although he said Emily had indicated that the stalking had stopped, so maybe she didn't feel the need to go into the specifics of the email. Did you find anything else?"

"Yes, I also found another set of emails that Suzanne Gordon sent to her that I want you to read. The content bothers me. Luke read them and feels the same way. I can email them to you, but I'd rather you read them here at the station while I'm with you. I don't want to say much more until I see you in person. By the way, I talked with the ME earlier. He's completed the autopsy."

"What did he find?"

"Emily's skull was fractured, and there were metal splinters embedded in it. He believes they may be cast iron but sent them to the crime lab in Rochester for verification. Her neck and lots of bones were also broken."

"What actually killed her?"

"Inconclusive," Carrie answered. "If she had had immediate medical attention, she probably wouldn't have died from the skull fracture, but if that didn't kill her the broken neck certainly would have. We need to find whatever it was that caused the skull fracture since it certainly set things in motion to cause her death. When will you be back?"

"I want to call Annie to check in, then I'll be on my way. The roads have been cleared, so I should be there in an hour. I'll meet you at the station. Oh, and since I've talked with Jonathan Bradford, you can notify the media to let them know who the deceased is. I remember you got them to agree to go with the story but withhold Emily's name from the report until we talked to next of kin."

"I'll take care of it. See you soon."

Ed called Annie, but she wasn't answering either her cell phone or the house landline. She took yoga at Suzanne's studio a couple of afternoons each week, and he figured she probably was at a class. He left a message on both phones that he would be meeting with

Carrie when he got back to Lighthouse Cove and if she hadn't prepared dinner yet to plan to go out since he wasn't sure how long he would be.

Chapter 16

It was dark by the time Ed arrived at the police station. He declined the coffee Carrie offered, knowing that by now, unless it was freshly brewed, it was probably thick as tar and impossibly bitter. Instead, he accepted a cup of hot tea.

"The crime lab just called and verified that the splinters embedded in Emily's head are pieces of cast iron," she said, "but we still don't know what hit her. There are some cast iron pieces in the museum, but most of them are big and heavy, like anchors, which wouldn't be easy to pick up. There were no identifiable fingerprints or other evidence on them, so it may be that the weapon belonged to the perp. Also, we found some dark, curly hairs on Emily's coat that clearly are not hers. Suzanne has dark curly hair. Please read the emails and let me know what you think." She then gave him a summary of what was in them.

After listening to her interpretation, Ed agreed the emails might put suspicion on Suzanne, but also advised her not to over-react.

"I don't know Suzanne very well, and we don't know if the hairs on Emily's coat are hers. Even if they are, there could be a perfectly simple explanation for them being there. They were close friends," he reminded her. "Close friends sometimes hug. I think we need to proceed with caution."

Carrie argued, "Ed, I'm going to get a search warrant for Suzanne's house. I'll wait until tomorrow, though, since nothing much is going to happen tonight, we're both tired, and I don't think Judge Tyler would be too happy if we interrupted her dinner."

Ed stood up and stretched. "I know you're in charge of the investigation, Carrie, but I'd wait a bit before getting that warrant. Even if the emails cast some suspicion on Suzanne, what I'd like to do first is call her tomorrow and ask her to meet with me as a follow-up to our discussion on the day of the murder. I'll question her about them. If we're not happy with the results of that interview, then we can get a warrant. How's that sound?"

Carrie reluctantly agreed to Ed's suggestion, admitting that he trumped her on experience with murder investigations but then reiterated her belief that sometimes the least obvious were often the killers. "I've gotten way past the idea that killers look and act a certain way or fit a certain profile."

"Do you still want to stay here while I read the emails, Carrie, or would you rather go home?"

"I'll stay. You seem to believe that I'm over-reacting, but since you haven't read them you really don't know that," Carrie testily replied.

Ed ignored Carrie's last remark and sat down at the computer, but just as he started to read, he slapped his palm against his forehead.

"I completely forgot that I wanted to ask you something. Annie found a gold, anchor-shaped pendant at the museum. It was monogrammed with the museum's initials, but she didn't recognize it as anything from the gift shop, although she surmised it might have been something Emily had recently purchased and hadn't yet packaged. She gave it to Luke who said he'd turn it over to you. Was there anything on it that we can use?"

"Sorry, I forgot to mention it to you. Luke did turn it in, and I sent it to the techs in Rochester for analysis.

They didn't find anything that would link it to the murder."

"Too bad. I was hoping that maybe it would be another piece of evidence," responded Ed.

"It's not, and we have no further need to keep it. I haven't had time to return it to Annie. If I give it to you, will you make sure she gets it?"

Ed nodded as Carrie opened her desk drawer and pulled out a plastic bag containing the pendant. Ed removed the piece from the bag, examined it, and put it in his pocket. "There's something about this that's familiar," he said to Carrie. His eyes narrowed. "I think I've seen it somewhere before. Not at the museum, but somewhere else. I just can't remember where." Then he started reading.

Chapter 17

From the E-Mails of Emily Bradford and Suzanne Gordon:

"Dear Emily,

Please believe me when I tell you I have only your best interests at heart. I know what I've asked of you seems a bit unseemly, but I think that until you deal with the demons that continue to haunt you, and with your ambivalent feelings, you won't be able to heal and move on with your life. You know how much I care for you and am concerned about you.

Love,
Suzanne"

"Dear Suzanne,

I know how much you care for me and completely understand why you think moving in with you may be a good idea, but I'm just not ready to do that. I know you mean well, but I need time alone to look at the circumstances that got me where I am and ways I can move forward and live more authentically.

Love,
Emily"

"Dear Emily,

My only purpose is to give you support while you are still struggling to resolve your issues. If you come and stay with me, and, at some point, decide it's not right for you, I can handle that. (-:

Love,
Suzanne"

"Dear Suzanne,

I just can't. Your offer, while well-intentioned, is misguided. Being with you might only make things worse. What I mostly need now is solitude and time.

Best,
Emily"

"Dear Emily,

I understand you're struggling and am sorry you won't change your mind. All I want is for you to resolve your conflicts and gain clarity, and I'm willing to take this step if it helps you be who I know you can be and come to a place of peace and understanding.

Love,
Suzanne"

"The emails stop there," Carrie said.

"Interesting," Ed said. "What bothers you about these?"

Carrie responded, "While it's certainly possible that Suzanne wanted Emily to stay with her because she was troubled about her emotional well-being, I'm wondering if what was really going on was that Suzanne was in love with Emily and that Emily had some pretty strong feelings for her but couldn't come to terms with it. That perhaps she was conflicted about her own sexuality."

"I didn't read anything like that in those emails, Carrie. They seem to be written out of concern for her friend. We don't know a thing about Suzanne's sexual orientation, and even if she were in love with Emily and Emily was struggling with her own feelings, it's a really long stretch to think the conflict would result in her murder."

"Ed, you have to admit these could cast some suspicion on her."

"I'm not seeing them that way at all, Carrie. Suzanne seems to be very grounded and an emotionally healthy person, and Annie, who's a very good judge of character, speaks very highly of her. I think the emails were written from one caring and supportive friend to another who was experiencing a lot of emotional distress."

"But if Suzanne killed Emily, it might not have been premeditated," argued Carrie. "Maybe Suzanne knew that Emily was going to go to the museum early the day of the board meeting and went there to talk with her in person and try to persuade her to change her mind. Maybe they got into an argument, and in the heat of the moment Suzanne pushed Emily and she fell against something made of cast iron, a tragic accident that killed her."

"You're grasping at straws, Carrie," Ed responded, impatiently. "If that had been the case, why wouldn't Suzanne have called 911? Since it would have been an accident, she wouldn't have been criminally charged, and Emily might still be living. She obviously cared for her," Ed responded.

"Even if it was an accident and she didn't mean to kill her, maybe when she realized what had happened she couldn't face it so in a panic threw Emily over the bluff, and then staged the whole break-in at the museum as a cover up," Carrie insisted.

"She's strong and very fit, so it wouldn't have been impossible. The locks weren't picked, and Suzanne is one of the board members who has a key to the museum."

"Let's see how my interview with her goes," Ed suggested, weary from the long day and tired of arguing, "and then decide after that if we should get a warrant."

"Okay, Ed, I'll wait, but I'm still going to order a background check on her. That way we'll cover all our bases."

Ed said, "I think ordering a background check is premature, Carrie, but you need to do what you feel is right. I'll call you and let you know when I'm meeting with her. I'm going to let her choose the location rather than asking her to come to the station. It might be less threatening for her."

Chapter 18

Annie was shutting down her computer when Ed got home. She'd been updating a spreadsheet of museum volunteers' names and contact information. "Hard day?" she asked. Ed's face was drawn, and he looked exhausted.

Ed sighed, "Long and very difficult day, and I'm tired. All the people who I thought could be suspects aren't. Jon Bradford had a perfect alibi and truly seemed distraught about Emily's death, the dean at the university was adamant that none of her colleagues or students would have any motive whatsoever for wanting her dead, a former lover died several months ago of cancer, and I even checked out his widow, who while one of the most self-righteous people I've ever encountered, didn't have a motive either.

"There's someone living here in Lighthouse Cove who Carrie thinks could be a suspect. She found what she believes are suspicious emails between that person and Emily, so I'm going to call tomorrow and schedule an interview. I'm not able to tell you who it is right now, especially since the evidence is very circumstantial, but also because I think Carrie is way off base on this one."

"When you withhold info from me you have your reasons," Annie responded. "I've seen you work on so many murder cases that I know you have to be discreet and often can't give me all the details until you have solid evidence, so I won't press you."

"Thanks for understanding."

"You're welcome. Ed, I didn't get your message until after I'd already prepared dinner for tonight. I made a huge pot of Tuscan tomato soup and bought a wedge of Asiago cheese and some good crusty bread before I went to yoga. If you're too tired to go out, we can stay in. If you still want to go, the meal will keep until tomorrow."

"You know, I've been so focused on this murder for the past couple of days, and so preoccupied, that even though I'm exhausted I think I would like to go out tonight and do something fun. It'll be a nice change."

"Would you have a problem with the Beauvoirs joining us? I ran into Eve at yoga today, and she asked if we might want to meet her and Henri at The Brewery for dinner. There's an acoustical guitar player performing. I told her I'd text her and let her know one way or the other, but whatever you prefer is fine with me."

"It would be nice to catch up with good friends. Go ahead and text Eve and let her know we'll meet them, how about in an hour? I'd like to shower and change my clothes." Annie picked up her cell phone off the kitchen counter and texted her friend.

"Annie," Ed continued, "I'd like this evening to be as low key as possible. I'm aware that everyone in the village is talking about the murder, but I'd rather not say too much about it, so if Eve or Henri or anyone else we run into asks, I'm just going to tell them we have a couple of leads but nothing concrete yet and then change the subject. Is that okay with you?"

"Of course, Ed."

"Now that's enough about me. How was your day? Did Carrie give you the okay to go into the basement?"

"She did and agreed that Luke could come with me and help me bring some boxes here."

"Did you find anything valuable?"

"After I got there I changed my mind and decided that going into that cold dark basement today just didn't appeal to me. Emily's death has upset me more than I realized. Luke was waiting for me on the front porch, and I told him what I'd decided but asked him if he'd allow me to go in and check for phone messages and go through the mail. He said I could, but that I couldn't touch anything else and should bring the mail back here, so I wouldn't contaminate the scene. He didn't think he needed to stay with me so long as I was willing to leave as soon as I was finished and was comfortable being there by myself. I was and sent him back to the police station with a promise to have him over for dinner some night when things settle down."

"You stayed by yourself? You certainly remember that I didn't want you to do that right now, Annie," Ed admonished.

"I only stayed for a little while longer, Ed. You're being overprotective, and I'm not a child."

"Maybe it's his inexperience, Annie, but Luke was not using good judgment."

"You're over-reacting. Luke cautioned me to lock the door and stood outside and watched me turn the dead bolt before leaving," Annie, frustrated and angry, said tersely.

Ed sighed. "Maybe I am over-reacting, but it's just out of concern."

Exasperated, she sighed, shook her head and continued, "Anyway, after I gathered up the mail, I went to the phone with the answering machine which is on Emily's desk. There were some messages on it that were too extensive for me to input into the notes app on my cell phone. I needed paper to write them down and figured the top drawer of her desk probably had a pad or some sticky notes and a pen.

"The drawer was partially open and when I opened it the whole way, I found a broken chain stuck in the crack of the side of the drawer. I pulled it out without thinking, but after I realized what I'd done decided it might be evidence, so I called Luke and stayed there until he came back to retrieve it. He wasn't happy that I didn't listen to him and went into the desk without permission but said that in the long run, because of what I'd found, he wouldn't make a big deal of it. He said Carrie would send it to the crime lab."

"Annie, Luke's right. You shouldn't have done that, but if the chain can be linked to the murder, maybe it's a good thing you did. Though I am a bit miffed that the techs didn't find it. First the anchor, now the chain. It seems to me that they should have been more thorough."

"Do you remember what the museum looks like, Ed?" countered Annie impatiently. "It's trashed. I think they did the best they could when they went through the building the first time but missed a couple of things. Remember, Luke said they planned to do a final run-through today and I expect, if I hadn't found the pendant and chain, they would have."

"Let's hope that's true, Annie. While you did the right thing by calling Luke, you're not off the hook. You shouldn't be spending time alone in the museum right now."

"I'm not going to argue with you, Ed," Annie scoffed. "As you can see, I was fine, and as soon as the techs are out of there for good, I intend to spend time at my office when I want to."

Resigned to having a feisty and independent wife, Ed shook his head and went upstairs to clean up. Half-an-hour later he came down the steps looking refreshed and feeling much calmer. He and Annie decided that a brisk walk would do them both good, so wearing jeans, heavy sweaters, ski parkas, mittens, and boots that crunched through a sparkling layer of newly fallen snow, they headed towards the restaurant, engaging in idle chatter and avoiding any discussion about the murder case.

Inside The Brewery an open hearth fire was roaring, and the noise volume, made louder by the high, wood-beamed ceiling, reflected the large and diverse crowd that had gathered for pizza, wings, and adult beverages, and to listen to the guitar performance.

Sturdy round oak tables with wide-bottomed captain's chairs filled the cavernous room that was framed at one end by a polished wooden horseshoe-shaped bar where their friends, Eve and Henri, sat—he, drinking dark ale, and she, a white wine. Both were munching on popcorn from a basket that the bartender had placed before them.

Ed ordered a glass of red wine for Annie, a single malt scotch for himself, and after several minutes the hostess led the two couples to a table near the fireplace and close to where the guitar player had set up. As predicted, several diners came over to the table to talk about the murder, but Ed deftly changed the subject after telling them the investigation had produced few leads.

Chapter 19

Black, mainly black, with tan and green and occasional flashes of white lightening swirled through the air with cries of anguish and lots of buzzing, buzzing, buzzing that got louder, so much so that it awakened the dreamer just as the 10 p.m. edition of the evening news started airing on the TV that had been on since late that afternoon.

While Ed and Annie were saying goodbye to their friends after spending several pleasant hours munching on pizza and wings and tapping their feet to the folk music of the acoustical guitar player, Emily's murderer, now fully awake after having passed out on the sofa from drinking a half bottle of vodka a couple of hours earlier, stood up and started pacing back and forth while the perky, trim brunette news anchor gave an update on the murder at the Lighthouse Cove museum and named the victim, indicating that the police had exhausted all obvious leads but still were looking for clues that would help them find her killer. She reported that there now was reason to believe that someone may have targeted Emily Bradford and purposely made the crime look like a burglary gone awry.

"It's not my fault; this was not my fault," her killer moaned. "Things just got out of control, and they shouldn't have. I never wanted this to happen. She shouldn't have screamed at me. If she hadn't screamed none of this would have happened."

In a fit of frustration and rage, the killer kicked over the side table, upsetting the liquor bottle and spilling its remaining contents on the floor. Mopping the puddle up with a hastily retrieved roll of paper towels and shaking with nervous tension, the killer repeated a mantra several times, "I have to pull myself together. I have to calm down."

Chapter 20

The snow had stopped and the sky, now clean and clear, sparkled with a multitude of stars so bright that Ed and Annie could easily identify many of the constellations. As waves softly lapped against the shore they walked home, arm-in-arm, talking quietly. Ed admitted that going out for pizza with their friends had helped take his mind off the investigation and made him feel calmer and less edgy than he had for the past couple of days.

"Since leaving Albany and especially since I retired as police chief here, I've missed the challenges related to crime-solving on an ongoing rather than part-time basis as a consultant. I must admit that being hired to help solve this murder has been giving me somewhat of an adrenaline rush. But slowing down tonight and having a bit of normalcy, even if just for a few hours, has been good for me, and I think probably for us since we've had a little time to connect without constantly focusing on Emily's death and the break-in," he said.

"I'm glad this evening helped you, Ed. I know how much you want to solve Emily's murder, but you're not a youngster any more, and being obsessed 24/7 can't be good for your health. I've been very concerned about you. While you're in great shape, please remember that you are in your 60s."

A little later as they snuggled in bed, Ed yawned and said to Annie, "Tonight was a lot of fun, but you're right, I do sometimes forget I'm in my 60s. I just realized how exhausted I am and hope I'll be able to

sleep tonight. Carrie and I have a long day ahead of us."
He kissed Annie, told her he loved her and appreciated
her support, closed his eyes and was asleep within
minutes.

Chapter 21

At 8:30 the next morning Suzanne's phone rang, just as she was entering her house after her morning walk. She needed to get into the shower to get ready for work and almost let the message line pick up but at the last second decided to answer it, hoping whomever was on the line would be brief.

"Hello, this is Suzanne. May I help you?" she asked, a melodious Jamaican lilt in her voice.

"Good morning, Suzanne. It's Ed DeCleryk."

"Hello, Ed. What can I do for you?"

"I'd like to do a follow-up to the interview we had the day of Emily's murder, Suzanne, and I'm hoping you'll be able to meet with me sometime today."

"I don't know what more I can add, Ed, but certainly I'll meet with you. I'll do whatever is necessary to help you find Emily's killer. When and where would you like to meet?"

"Any time and place that's convenient for you. Your house, your wellness center, Bistro Louise or the police station if that works best since it's located right across the street from your center."

"I wanted to get to my office to do some planning and paperwork before my first class. But that isn't until 11:00, and I can put the paperwork on hold. Why don't you stop over in about an hour? I just got back from a walk, and that will give me time to clean up. I'll brew some tea, and we can chat. Would that work?"

"That's perfect," Ed responded. "See you soon."

He hung up the phone and called Carrie who expressed disappointment that Suzanne hadn't suggested meeting Ed at the police station since she was hoping to listen in on the conversation.

"I'll ask Suzanne if she would mind my recording our interview, just so I don't forget any details. I can't imagine she'd refuse, and then you can listen to it when I get back," Ed offered.

An hour later, Ed walked up three steps to Suzanne's front porch and knocked on the door. The small Victorian cottage, painted indigo blue with white gingerbread trim, backed up onto a narrow canal that spilled into the bay. Opening the lime-green door, Suzanne greeted him and motioned him inside where colorful steel drum art decorated the walls along with stunning seascapes, done in muted watercolors. Accent walls of vivid blue, lime green and mango set a welcoming backdrop to simple upholstered white twill furniture. Spices lined a shelf along one wall of the small kitchen, with cookbooks set on windowsills and countertops.

They had just sat down and started to talk when they heard a loud crash. Startled by the noise, Ed jumped. Suzanne laughed.

"Oh, that's just Matilda," she said. Just then a huge tabby cat walked into the room. "Matilda likes to sleep on the dressing table in my bedroom," she explained.

"When she heard us talking and didn't recognize your voice she probably decided to see who was visiting, and when she jumped off the table she knocked something onto the floor. It happens all the time." Ed smiled, looking very sheepish.

After settling in with a cup of tea, Ed asked Suzanne if she minded if he recorded the interview. "I'll want to share it with Carrie and don't want to forget anything."

Suzanne pursed her lips together and then quietly asked, "Am I a suspect? Do I need an attorney?"

Ed responded quickly, "Of course not. The last thing I want is for you to feel threatened by this interview, and if you become uncomfortable you can end it at any time. But I don't want to forget any of our conversation when I report to Carrie about it, since she's directing the investigation."

Suzanne consented, and Ed, to put her at ease, began with small talk, asking her questions about her background and how she came to open her practice in Lighthouse Cove.

She answered that she'd been a trained therapist practicing in Rochester when she started feeling burned out from dealing with clients who came to her when their lives, full of stress, had already cascaded out of control. After much reflection, she determined she wanted to deal with mental and emotional health issues in a more positive way and closed her practice.

"I decided that rather than helping repair the damage done to my clients in the aftermath of stress in their lives, I could be more effective by doing preventive work and helping people learn ways to live healthier lives before stress made them ill."

She said she and her family had spent many weekends in Lighthouse Cove when she was a teenager, loving it for its beauty and serenity, which is why she chose to move and open her wellness center in the village. Its proximity to Rochester also enabled her to have ongoing contact with her family and friends there.

"Annie may have mentioned that I offer nutritional counseling, teach yoga and meditation, do therapeutic massage, and conduct wellness seminars." Ed nodded.

"Is that how you met Emily? Did she take one of your classes?" Ed asked, segueing to the purpose of his visit.

Suzanne shook her head. "Shortly after I moved to Lighthouse Cove I got involved as a volunteer at the museum, and that was how we met. We started walking together each morning, along with my next-door neighbor, Mary Ellen Vanderline, and eventually became good friends."

"Did you walk the morning of the murder?" he asked, leading into the questioning.

"Yes, but Emily didn't walk with us. We'd had dinner the night before, but she wanted to go to the museum before the board meeting to get some work done and set up the coffee. Because I had the meeting at 9 a.m. and Mary Ellen had made plans to go to Canandaigua with her husband, Leslie, for the day to watch their grandchildren, we were out earlier than normal, about 6:30. It was still dark. We walked for about 45 minutes and then stopped at the Bistro for lattes and croissants. I got home about 8 a.m., showered, changed and then drove to the museum for the meeting."

"Did you go by the museum when you walked and if so, do you remember seeing anything that looked suspicious?" Ed asked.

Suzanne explained that they normally did walk by the museum, but because they were a bit short on time skipped that part of the route that day.

"When you had dinner did Emily seem nervous or jumpy? Was there anything about her behavior that struck you as odd?" Ed asked.

"That night Emily seemed fine, but I've been concerned about her for a long time. She had a lot going on in her life and suffered from some anxiety and depression. I was keeping a close eye on her."

"What was causing Emily such distress?" Ed asked.

"I believe I mentioned when you interviewed me the morning of the murder that her parents died in a tragic accident. I can't remember if I also said she was separated from her husband, Jon, and that she had resigned her position from the university because of an affair with a student."

"You alluded to her parents' deaths," Ed responded. "I learned more about that tragedy and about her affair and marital status from some other sources."

Suzanne continued, "Her marriage had been rocky for several months before the affair started, but the separation occurred because of it. She felt terribly guilty. I was also concerned she might be starting to suffer from seasonal affective disorder, which, because of the lack of sun and short days in winter, is quite common in our part of the world.

"I recommended she increase her vitamin D, gave her some herbal supplements, suggested diet changes, and got her to take one of my yoga classes."

"Was that helping or was she getting worse?" Ed asked, wondering if, instead of being murdered, Emily had become despondent and had thrown herself over the bluff, striking her head on some debris made from cast iron before she hit the beach, and that the break-in at the museum had been coincidental.

Suzanne shook her head. "The supplements and classes were helping a little; she didn't seem quite as depressed."

She continued, "Still, I thought she needed professional help to work through her issues. Since we were friends, I didn't feel as though I could serve in the role of a therapist for her but suggested she see a friend of mine who practices in the city. She was mulling it over."

Ed got straight to the point, "Carrie and Luke were at her house yesterday and found the emails you wrote and wondered about their content. Was it because of her emotional state that you asked her to live with you? Were you that concerned?"

"I wasn't worried she would harm herself in the short run, but I was concerned that with winter coming her depression might worsen. She's very isolated out there on the peninsula, plus most of her neighbors are gone for the season and with the heavy snow we get out here, getting into the city on a regular basis to see her friends who live there isn't always easy.

"I kept in touch, but there were days when I didn't have time to visit with her because of my schedule at the wellness center. I thought if she could stay with me awhile she might feel more supported and would continue to heal. She refused, telling me she was starting to work out her problems and that she didn't need a babysitter."

"Ouch," responded Ed.

"I knew I'd hit a sore spot, and her reaction was pretty much as I expected. But I felt I had to try."

Thinking about his advice to Carrie the day before about not jumping to conclusions about the emails, Ed felt vindicated. Suzanne's explanation about them made sense. But she hadn't explained why she'd withheld information about Emily's affair when he'd interviewed her the first time.

Ed said, "I learned about Emily's affair with Eric Sewall through other sources, but I'm wondering why you didn't tell me about it when I questioned you on the day of the murder."

"I'd lost a beloved friend and was distraught. And I was trying to comfort Charles Merrill who seemed to feel strongly that Emily had been killed during a botched burglary attempt, so I expect that's what I assumed as well. I also knew, because Emily had confided in me, that Eric had sent her an email apologizing for the stalking and letting her know he wouldn't be bothering her again. I didn't say anything to you because I didn't have any reason to think he might be implicated in Emily's murder."

"You didn't know he'd died?"

"He's dead?" She gasped, and her eyes widened. "Oh, my God. Was he murdered? Does his death have something to do with Emily's? Or did he commit suicide? Emily told me he was unstable. If she knew Eric had died that certainly could have impacted her emotionally."

"He didn't commit suicide, and he wasn't murdered. We don't think Emily knew. We learned he'd died of cancer several months ago."

Suzanne sighed and shook her head.

Starting another line of questioning, Ed asked, "What restaurant did you go to the night before she was killed? Did you notice anything out of the ordinary, anyone who looked suspicious?"

She answered, "We didn't go out. Emily came here to the house. She liked to cook, and I invited her over to learn how to prepare red snapper with lime and coconut. It's a popular Jamaican dish."

"Was she more upset or tense than usual or worried about anything?"

Suzanne shook her head. "Not at all. Everything seemed fine. In fact, Emily was very relaxed, the best she'd been for a long time."

"Did she drive to your house?" Ed asked, wondering if perhaps someone had followed her.

"No, she didn't. As you know, my wellness center is only a few blocks from her house. Her car was in the shop, so I told her I'd swing by and pick her up after work and then bring her home after dinner."

"Did anyone else join you for dinner or were the two of you alone?"

"The dish we were going to cook serves four to six, so at the last minute I invited my boyfriend, Garrett Rosenfeld, and one of his law partners, Sheila Caldwell, who is also a friend of mine. Her spouse was working that night so couldn't join us."

"And you can't think of anything that happened that was unusual?"

"No, absolutely not. We had a wonderful evening with lots of wine and laughter and had just finished eating when my dad called. He owns a Caribbean restaurant, Callaloo, in the city, and his hostess had asked for Sunday off for some family situation. He wanted to know if I could come in and work for him that day. Sheila had brought her dog, Elmo, and while I was on the phone she went out to walk him, and Garrett and Emily started cleaning up the kitchen. I heard them talking and laughing while I was on the phone."

"When you drove her home, did you notice any strange cars or anyone lurking near her house?"

"I didn't drive her home. Garrett and Sheila dropped her off on their way back to Rochester. Before she left, she pulled me aside and said she had decided to get counseling and was hopeful she could work through her grief over her parents' death and her shame at the affair and reconcile with Jon. I hugged her and we both cried." Suzanne's eyes welled up, and she dabbed at them with a tissue.

"Do Garrett and Sheila know about her murder?"

"Yes. I called them. Emily's death is no secret and I didn't want them to find out through the news. They are very upset. I asked Garrett if he noticed anything unusual when he took Emily home, but he said he didn't. He said he walked her to the door and waited until she was safely inside to go back to his car. You might want to talk with him anyway. And Sheila.

Maybe they'll remember something that they didn't think of before."

"Good suggestion. Is there anything else you think I should know?"

Suzanne shook her head.

"Then I won't keep you any longer." He turned off the recorder, stood up and clasped her hands in his.

"Thank you so much. I don't know if our conversation will get us any closer to finding Emily's murderer, but you certainly have helped me understand the sequence of events that night."

Chapter 22

Ed met Carrie at the police station and played the interview for her.

"Garrett Rosenfeld is Suzanne's boyfriend?" Carrie asked.

"You know him?"

"No, not personally. I took a continuing education course in criminal justice last year at Finger Lakes Community College, and he was one of the instructors. He's a defense attorney and was a fabulous lecturer. I learned a lot."

"So, what's your take on the interview?" asked Ed.

"After listening to it, it's obvious she didn't kill Emily," responded Carrie. "I was way off base about their relationship and the reason for the emails. And you're right, even if the curly hairs on Emily's coat were Suzanne's, they were close friends who spent a lot of time together, and Suzanne did say they hugged before Emily left. Still, it's one more lead down the tubes. Maybe our original premise, that Emily was in the wrong place at the wrong time, is the accurate one, Ed, and she really was the victim of an unpremeditated murder, despite our recent assumption that someone had targeted her."

"I agree," responded Ed. "And now that we've finished, I'd like to take a break. You seem to have things under control, and I need to work on an agenda for a meeting I'm chairing tonight for the Silver Bay Association. Are you okay if I go home and do that?"

"Sure. I'll call Suzanne's boyfriend, Garrett, and her friend, Sheila, to see if they remember anything and call you when Suzanne's background check comes in. I don't expect there will be anything in it that will be a problem. Go home and put some normalcy in your life. I'll talk with you later." She paused. "I'm sorry I was so testy yesterday."

"You just want to find Emily's killer, Carrie. We all do. Apology accepted."

*****

Carrie called Ed mid-afternoon. "I talked with Garrett and Sheila. Neither of them could remember anything unusual that would help us solve Emily's murder. I also got the results of Suzanne's background check. She's so clean she squeaks and hasn't even had a parking or speeding ticket."

"I'm not surprised. But with Suzanne no longer a person of interest, it looks like we've come to a dead end in terms of suspects. As you said earlier, Carrie, it may be that Emily was in the wrong place at the wrong time and the victim of a bungled burglary. We have no murder weapon, no suspicious prints or other evidence. We don't even know if the break-in was premeditated or random, perhaps a druggie looking for money or valuables. We may never find Emily's killer."

"I don't want to close the case, Ed, but you're probably right. Someone may have committed the perfect crime."

Chapter 23

Three days later, on a bright sunny day following a brief service at the white-spired Episcopal Church located in the village, Emily Bradford was buried on a hill overlooking Silver Bay, her grave site flanked by two ancient weeping willows, denuded of leaves, stems hanging down like cascades of amber colored tears. A light layer of ice on the water reflected the sun's rays, creating a rainbow of shimmering colors on the bay's surface. The grass was covered with unblemished white snow that contrasted sharply with the cloudless, cobalt sky.

Jon Bradford, his parents, siblings and their families had been followed from the church to the cemetery by a long procession that included Suzanne, her boyfriend, Garrett, Ed and Annie, as well as neighbors, colleagues, students and former students, winery employees, and museum board members, all wanting to pay their respects.

Charles Merrill had attended the church service, but not feeling well, had gone home instead of to the cemetery where the large crowd stood in somber reflection as the minister led the group in additional prayers and hymns. One young man, subdued, weeping and dressed head to toe in black, stood apart from the rest of the group, and Ed guessed he had been one of Emily's students.

After the casket was lowered into the ground, the mourners headed to their cars in silence. Ed and Annie caught up with Suzanne, who introduced the couple to a tall, clean-shaven, brown-haired man with olive skin and arresting eyes the color of cognac.

"This is my friend, Garrett Rosenfeld," she said.

Ed and Annie shook hands with Garrett and told him they were pleased to meet him despite the sad circumstances, then turning to Suzanne, Ed said, "Tough day, Suzanne. I know how much you loved Emily and hope the interview the other day didn't cause you too much distress."

"It's no problem, Ed. You were only doing your job," Suzanne replied. "I'm just sorry I couldn't think of anything that would help you get closer to discovering how and why Emily was killed. I must confess that when you called and asked to interview me again I was terrified, and then became more so when you asked to record it. I guess I've watched enough movies and TV programs to know that sometimes innocent people are charged and found guilty of crimes they didn't commit. I was scared witless that your real agenda for talking with me was that I was a suspect and I'd end up being charged with murder."

"I regret my interview with you was so stressful, Suzanne," responded Ed.

"I've lost a good friend," Suzanne responded. "I'm sad, angry and very upset and need to take some time to grieve. Will you need to interview me again?" Ed shook his head.

"Good. I won't be able to get through the grieving process if I'm constantly reminded of what happened to Emily. Now if you'll excuse me, Garrett and I want to talk a bit with Jonathan's family."

Annie hugged Suzanne, and Ed stood by looking very somber as she walked away from them, holding hands with Garrett, her shoulders sagging.

As Ed and Annie walked towards their car, a tall, distinguished looking man with dark hair, graying at the temples, wearing a black cashmere overcoat and soft black leather gloves strode over to them and introduced himself.

"I'm Gerard Bradford, Jon's father," he said, extending his hand first to Annie and then to Ed while looking directly at them with quiet blue-gray eyes. "We are devastated by Emily's death; she was like a daughter to my wife and me, and we had always hoped she and Jon would reconcile. I understand you have no leads."

Ed shook his head. "Unfortunately, we don't. We've run into a complete dead end. We are back to thinking it was a burglar who must have been surprised to discover Emily in the building, and after striking her and throwing her body over the bluff, left without taking a thing. It might be someone who was looking for money or something he could pawn, possibly to pay for drugs, so it may have been an act of desperation. If that's the case, he could strike again, probably not at our museum, but possibly at others. This time of year, unless there's heightened security, it wouldn't be that difficult to do since we live in such a remote area of upstate New York. We've informed all the police departments along the lake, and they've increased their patrols and will let us know if anything suspicious occurs in their communities."

Bradford reached into his pocket, pulled out a business card and handed it to Ed. "Could you please keep me posted? Our family has lots of resources so if you need anything at all, private investigators, funds for additional security or to pay for accommodations if you need to travel to check out a lead, please let me know. We all want to find Emily's killer and have him put away for life."

Ed thanked him, pulled out one of his own business cards and gave it to Gerard with a promise to stay in touch.

Chapter 24

A few days before Thanksgiving, Ben Fisher called Carrie and told her that his return to Lighthouse Cove would be delayed, most likely until after the holiday. His father-in-law was hanging on, and he and his wife didn't want to fly back to Lighthouse Cove only to have to return to Arizona for the funeral. Carrie filled him in on the investigation, and he concurred with her that Emily's death may have been the result of her being in the wrong place at the wrong time and that, if by the time he returned, there were no suspects or no arrests, he might close the case, not having the resources to continue it.

By Thanksgiving the snow had melted, and the sun shone brightly with fluffy white clouds casting shadows on the serene steel blue lake. The DeCleryks, their two sons and daughters-in-law and five grandchildren celebrated the holiday with hikes on the beach where gentle waves lapped the shore, board games, and for the little ones, a game of hide and seek through the rambling house.

As usual, Annie had invited friends and acquaintances without families in the area to join them for the meal, including Charles Merrill, who said he'd made other plans.

Carrie's husband, Matt, was on call that weekend which made it impossible for them to visit their families, who lived on Long Island and in Brooklyn. They, too, declined Annie's invitation telling her they wanted to spend a quiet day at home together. Annie had also checked with Luke, who said he was going to Connecticut to spend the holiday with his parents and siblings, and with Suzanne who told her that she and her friend, Garrett, would be joining her parents, siblings and their families in Rochester at Callaloo, which was closed to the public for the holiday.

Chapter 25

More promising leads didn't pan out. A few days
after Thanksgiving, Chief Ben Fisher, now back from
Arizona after attending his father-in-law's funeral, got a
call from the police chief in Cooperstown, where a
burglar had been intercepted trying to get into the
Baseball Hall of Fame. Initial questioning revealed he
had planned to steal rare baseball cards to pawn for
drug money. Several hours later, Ben learned he had an
airtight alibi the night of the murder at the Lighthouse
Cove museum: he'd been incarcerated by the police in
nearby Utica on a DUI charge.

The safe in the office of a marina located along the
lakeshore between Lighthouse Cove and Windy Point
had been broken into one night, the robbers taking
money plus items from the maritime shop in the same
facility. A couple of days later, two men were
apprehended after they were stopped on a routine traffic
violation and some of the missing items were found on
the back seat of the car. Further investigation revealed
that they had committed a string of other robberies
during the past several months, one of which had been
at a marina on Lake Erie in Pennsylvania during the
morning of Emily's murder.

In nearby Bristol Harbor, police responded to an
alarm at the Historical Society located there. By the
time they arrived, the burglar was gone, and they found
nothing missing and everything in order. The chief,
puzzled, told Ben that he'd keep him posted, but called
back laughing a couple of days later. The president of

the Society, on her way to a conference in Albany, had at the last minute decided to grab some brochures that lay on a table just inside the door. Using her key to get in, she forgot to disable the alarm, grabbed the brochures and made a quick exit, passing the police in her car on their way to the historic building.

Chapter 26

November turned into December, but no additional suspects surfaced that would help Ed and the police force solve Emily's murder. The Christmas season was ushered in the first Saturday of that month, and Ed and Annie collected their grandchildren, who lived in Rochester, to stand in the bracing cold with other villagers to watch the annual holiday parade. After the parade, the crowd gathered at the welcome center, which was decorated to look like a gingerbread house, to help trim the huge Fraser fir with ornaments crafted by elementary students.

A community chili party at the firehouse followed the ceremony, the cost of admission being new, unwrapped toys to be given to needy families. After the meal, the children visited with Santa and Mrs. Claus, hopped on fire trucks, played games, and shopped for presents at the fire company auxiliary's North Pole Elves' store.

Several evenings later, Ed and Annie, their friends the Beauvoirs, and Carrie and her husband, Matt, joined a group of carolers who, not deterred by several inches of snow that had fallen during the day, navigated the streets in boots and snowshoes, cheerfully singing traditional holiday melodies in front of homes and businesses and escaping afterward from the bitter cold into The Brewery where the owner provided free hot cider and cookies to the merrymakers.

Two days after Christmas, the entire DeCleryk clan left for a highly anticipated ten-day trip to Disney

World and the Caribbean cruise. They would miss the annual Lighthouse Cove New Year's Eve celebration with their friends, a time when families gathered at the community center to eat pizza and watch old movies, and adults without children frequented the local pubs to listen to bluegrass, folk music and oldies performed by live bands. At midnight, villagers congregated on the snow-covered beach, ringed with bonfires, to view a stunning display of fireworks, followed by a pancake breakfast prepared by the neighborhood association.

Chapter 27

The DeCleryks returned to Lighthouse Cove the first
week in January. They'd enjoyed their trip but looked
forward to participating in the multitude of outdoor
activities villagers enjoyed on Silver Bay, which froze
14 inches deep during winter months.

Each Wednesday afternoon Ed joined a group of
other retirees who, keeping warm in makeshift huts
with smoky fires, cut holes in the ice and caught
steelhead trout, walleye, and perch. On Thursday
evenings, he and Annie rode their snowmobile across
the bay's hard, slick exterior to meet friends for dinner
at a bayside pub. One Sunday a month Annie
volunteered at the local hospital, and Ed competed in a
regional ice boat regatta, where sails unfurled, his sleek
boat raced against the wind across its glossy surface.

Annie was finally able to gather her docents together
to clean up the museum and put the artifacts back where
they belonged, and the board reconvened for its first
meeting of the year. Charles Merrill presided,
noticeably frailer than he had been before the holidays,
and with a slight tremor in both hands. Many of the
board members believed Emily's death had hit him the
hardest. The first order of business was to dedicate the
summer concert series to Emily's memory.

Martha and Patrick Kelly, a retired couple, offered to
co-run the gift shop in her place. The board also
approved the calendar of summer events which
included concerts in the park on Sunday afternoons, a
craft show, July 4 fireworks display; several sailing

regattas held in conjunction with the yacht club, breakfasts on the bluff, two ice cream socials and the annual triathlon competition.

Annie, now free to speak about Emily's intention to establish an endowment fund for the museum, reported that she had received a letter from Emily's law firm indicating that the paperwork had been completed before her death. She also reported that Gerard Bradford and his family had sent a large contribution with the stipulation that some of the money be used to install a security system with a numerical keypad system. The board voted to give Annie, Charles, Suzanne and additionally, the police chief, access to the code numbers.

Since many headed South in February to escape the worst of the winter, the board wasn't scheduled to meet again until March. Just before the meeting adjourned, Charles announced that when his term as president was over at the end of June he planned to resign from the board, so he could return to Canada where some relatives still lived, and he could receive free health care. He told them a mild heart condition had worsened, and that he'd also developed Parkinson's disease, thus the tremor in his hands. No one knew what to say, and the meeting ended on a very somber note.

That month Annie completed the gift inventory assessment for the museum, sent contracts to local artists and artisans and ordered gift items from several catalogues.

Chapter 28

The same morning that Annie and her crew were cleaning up the museum, Ben Fisher called Ed and told him he wanted to discuss the investigation with him and Carrie, and they arranged to meet in his office at eleven o'clock.

When Ed entered, Ben was sitting, feet up on his desk, chomping on an unlit cigar and looking pensive. Ed noticed a copy of *The Great Lakes Historical Times* in front of him.

Ed folded himself into a chair across from Ben. "Something you read in that got you thinking?" he asked, pointing at the magazine.

"Nah. I've been thinking about the case. The magazine has an article in it that Luke wanted me to read about shipwrecks on the lake. As you know, Annie's taken him under her wing and given him lots of reading material about the history of our region. As a result, he's become very interested in the lore of the sea. He wants to take some of his vacation time to go on a dive this summer with the Great Lakes Expedition. Seems they've found what they believe to be the remnants of a ship that went down just off our shores about 150 years ago."

"That might be a good fit for him, Ben. Other than trying to solve Emily's murder, our quiet village can't be providing him with many challenges."

At that moment, Carrie entered the office. "You wanted to see me, Chief?"

Ben motioned for her to sit. "I've been reviewing our investigation into Emily's murder. You and I talked around Thanksgiving, Carrie, about the possibility of shutting the investigation down if no more leads surfaced, and I think it may be time to do that."

He looked at Ed. "You've been very thorough, Ed, and I appreciate it, but it looks like the case has gone cold, and I can't keep paying you. I just don't have the money in our budget."

"I have to pull you away from the case as well, Carrie. I'm appointing you to serve on a joint taskforce of the Coast Guard and Homeland Security to look at implementing better security measures along the lakeshore"

He continued, "That's going to take some time along with your other responsibilities, and we need to have that done by May. As much as I'd like to, I just can't spare any more time trying to solve Emily's murder."

"With all due respect, sir, I disagree," argued Carrie. "I know it seems as though we've reached a dead end, but maybe we've missed something. Can't we just keep this open for a little while longer?"

"I wish we could, Carrie, but we can't. It's looking more and more plausible that Emily was killed in a botched burglary attempt. I'm not sure we'll ever find her killer. As sorry as I am to say this, we need to close this case." He waved his hand in dismissal. "I'll get back to you later this afternoon about that task force."

Ed and Carrie left the Chief's office and walked down the hall together.

Carrie said, "I'm very disappointed that he won't let us continue the investigation, Ed. I know in my gut that if we had more time we could solve Emily's murder."

Ed turned to Carrie and admitted he was as disappointed as she and still hoped at some point evidence would appear leading them to Emily's killer.

PART TWO
Chapter 29

No longer consulting for the Lighthouse Cove police department, Ed began accepting other jobs, including one in Albany where he assisted the police with a gun buy-back project and facilitated a training session there for rookie police officers. He and Annie took long walks, met friends for dinner, enjoyed outings with their children and grandchildren, and drove into the city to attend concerts and plays. They invited Luke to dinner twice, but each time he asked for a rain check saying he already had a commitment. Annie wondered if he were blowing them off and decided she would try once more, but if he declined again, she was going to let it drop.

Ed began renovating his classic sports car and continued restoring the old sailboat that had been sitting in his garage since the previous summer. He attended Bay Association and Rotary board meetings and met some of his retired Navy buddies who had settled in the area for a weekly lunch. Still, he continued to wonder if he and Carrie may have missed something when investigating Emily's murder.

One morning over breakfast in early February, Annie told Ed she thought she would go to the museum that day to start looking through the boxes in the basement.

"You're ready to do that? Do you need my help?" asked Ed.

"I am, plus it's got to be done. The basement is quite dark and will be cold, so yes, I could use your help in bringing them up to my office. I can go through them there. I'm expecting I'll find mostly junk, but I might discover something that's worth keeping."

Once inside the museum, Annie and Ed walked through Emily's former office, and Annie turned on a light at the top of the steep wooden steps that led to the basement. The gas furnace and water heater stood on thick, concrete pads placed over a dirt floor along the back wall at the bottom of the steps. The boxes had been stored in an adjacent room, where the only source of light was a bulb on the ceiling that was turned on by a pull string. Even after Annie turned it on, the shadows it cast made it difficult to see.

Sturdy metal shelves lined one wall, with large cardboard packing boxes stacked two or three each upon them. Ed walked towards the shelves and, because of the dim light, stubbed his toe on two that had been placed in the middle of the floor.

Exasperated, he groaned, "Annie, why would anyone leave these here on the floor?"

"I have no idea, Ed. When Donna gave me the building tour before she left to go back to England, I wasn't all that interested in coming down here. I decided I'd do it some other time, but it's never been a big priority."

The previous museum director, Donna Jones, had been born and raised in England and employed as the director of special projects for the Victoria and Albert Museum in London when her husband, a U.S. Air Force officer stationed at a base there, was reassigned to Fort Drum, in Watertown, NY.

Bored with attending teas and social events at the base, she conducted an online job search and learned about and applied for a position at the Lighthouse Cove

Museum. The museum board of directors, impressed with her credentials, offered her the position within a few days after interviewing her. She resided in the apartment above the museum, with her husband commuting from Watertown to join her on weekends. After a few years, her husband retired, and the couple returned to London where she was rehired at the museum where she'd worked before relocating to the States. She and Annie kept in touch.

Ed glanced around the room looking for anything else that might be out of place. In addition to a pile of dirt, he saw an old coal furnace, no longer in use; an empty coal bin and next to it, a cast iron coal scuttle. He bent down and peered closely at the scuttle, wondering if the techs had examined it for prints or evidence that might connect it to Emily's murder. He decided to not say anything to Annie until he thought it through a bit more.

"Would you like me to start with these two?" he asked, pointing to boxes on the floor.

"Please. We don't want anyone to trip over them like you almost did, plus even though the floor feels dry, it's dirt, so there must be some dampness. Hopefully nothing inside them has been ruined."

Ed lifted the first box off the floor and had turned towards the stairs when Annie spied a piece of paper, folded in half, on top of the second box. She picked it up and unfolded it. It looked like a copy of an old map, dated 1785 at the bottom.

"Wait a minute, Ed, look at this."

Ed walked back to Annie and peered at the map.

"Annie, I know how your imagination works, but before you get carried away, let me remind you that our kids attended a summer camp here years ago. It's probably a remnant from that. I seem to remember they conducted a big scavenger hunt at the end of the season for the campers where the last stop was a spot where they could dig for treasure that the counselors had buried."

"I know, Ed, but this looks more authentic than something a camp counselor drew. Look here, there's an X marking this spot. You can see the crescent beach, and here's the bluff plus the park and what appears to be a very primitive lighthouse on the edge of the bluff. Counselors would have drawn a map that depicts the current lighthouse and grounds. Maybe I'm way off base, but I'm wondering if there's any possibility this could be a copy of a real map. Remember, this entire property has been designated a national historic site."

"I wouldn't get your hopes up, Annie, but if your gut is telling you this might be a facsimile of a real map, you could check with some of the museum board members, especially those with knowledge about the early history of Lighthouse Cove, to see if anyone of them knows anything about this. Maybe they could tell you if there are rumors of buried treasure on this land."

Annie smiled. "Even though he's not been around here all that long, I might ask Charles to look at it. Before he moved here, he brushed up on the history of the southern shores of Lake Ontario. He's pretty much regarded as an expert, and he has resources to do some research. If he says there's nothing to it, so be it, but I'd be remiss in not showing it to him."

Annie carefully put the paper into the kangaroo pocket of her sweatshirt while Ed carried the first box upstairs and came back for the second. At first, the dim light obscured what was underneath the box, but as Annie glanced down she noticed a large hole beneath it, about two feet deep and 18 inches wide. "What in the world....!" she exclaimed.

Ed peered the hole. "Why would this be here, Annie?"

"I'm not sure, Ed, but I seem to remember Donna telling me there had been some plumbing problems with the building some years back," she responded.

"Maybe this is where the leak was, and the plumbers had to dig to find the damaged pipes to fix it. That might be where that pile of dirt came from. Then, for whatever reason, they didn't fill the hole, and someone put the boxes on top to prevent anyone from tripping and falling into it. I can get this filled in, but in the meantime, let's keep this second box on top of it for safety. Can you pull a couple from those shelves?"

Ed starting walking over to the shelves, but then stopped, looked at Annie and remarked, "It seems a little odd to me that someone wouldn't have the common sense to fill this." He glanced back at the dirt pile and at the coal scuttle.

"I know you and Donna keep in touch. Do you happen to have her contact information? I'd like to talk with her."

Annie laughed. "Really, Ed? Why do you want to talk with Donna? Oh my, you think this might have something to do with Emily's murder, don't you? What could Donna possibly know that could help you?"

"Yes, I'm wondering if there may be a connection to Emily's murder, but first I want to make sure it doesn't have anything to do with the plumbing problem. It's about four p.m. in England, so I can probably still catch Donna at work. If she's not there, I'll try and reach her on her cell phone. Do you have both numbers?"

Annie nodded, opened her contact file in her cell phone and gave Ed Donna's phone numbers.

"There won't be a good connection down here," he said. "I'll carry these boxes to your office and then stay there to make the call. If she's available, would you like to speak with her first?"

"I would."

A few minutes later, after chatting with Donna, Annie handed the phone back to Ed and sat cross-legged on the floor to open the boxes. He related to Annie, after ending the call, that Donna had no idea why the boxes were on the floor or why there was a hole under them. She was certain that the workmen didn't dig up any pipes.

Ed asked Annie, "When you were with the techs and Luke after the break-in, did anyone come down here looking for evidence or prints?"

"I remember one of them asking me if we had a basement, and I brought him over to the door and motioned to him to go down the steps. He didn't tell me that he'd found anything, but surely he would have mentioned it to you or Carrie if he had."

"He didn't say a word to me, or to Carrie as far as I know, so it's possible the tech found nothing suspicious. If those boxes were on the floor, it may have appeared to him that they belonged there, and like the rest of us, he may have assumed the crime was committed upstairs," Ed noted.

"But maybe that's a wrong assumption. Maybe someone was in the basement the morning Emily was killed, in the process of digging up something."

He continued, "Emily may have interrupted whatever that person was doing. It's possible she heard something in the basement and went down to investigate what the noise was. Not wanting to be discovered, the murderer picked up that coal scuttle and hit her with it, maybe just planning to knock her out so he could escape undetected. But he hit her hard enough to fracture her skull and when he saw what he'd done, he assumed he'd killed her, panicked, picked her up and threw her off the bluff, hoping that because it was still dark out and because of the high water and rough surf no one would find her for months, if ever. That's probably how her neck was broken and how she sustained all the other injuries. He must have figured she'd just go missing, crime never solved. He probably didn't see her coat and belongings in her office so didn't dispose of them, which is why Charles knew she'd been here."

"You think the coal scuttle could be the murder weapon, Ed? If that's true, then why wouldn't Emily's killer take it with him?"

"Your guess is as good as mine, Annie. He may have been wearing gloves so wasn't worried about his prints being on it. Or he may have been on foot and decided it was too awkward to carry, or in his haste to get out, just forgot about it.

"Coal scuttles are typically made of cast iron, so yes, I think it could be the murder weapon. If it was dusted for prints there were probably too many on it to provide any conclusive evidence and, as I said, the killer could have been wearing gloves. I'm going to take it over to the police station and ask that they get it over to the crime lab to see if the splinters they removed from Emily's head might be from the scuttle. I'm assuming they kept them along with other evidence in a cold case file. Why don't you come with me?"

"I'd like to stay here and finish this, Ed."

He expressed concern. "I'm still uneasy about you being here alone right now, Annie. Can't we agree that until the season starts you have someone with you when you're here? I'd feel much better about it."

"You're a dear man, Ed, and I know your concern is because you love me, but you're being really irrational," said Annie, giving him a withering look. "We've been through this before. It's plain daylight, and it's been a few months since Emily's murder. If the killer wanted to return to the museum, he would have done so already.

"If it was a random break-in and the burglar was looking for something he could pawn for money, he's not going to want to come back and risk getting caught, especially in broad daylight," she argued.

"Plus, we now have better security. I'll lock the door, and you can come get me when you're finished. I'll be fine." She grabbed a pencil and wrote some numbers on a piece of paper. "Here's the code to the keypad. You can let yourself in."

Ed reluctantly left the building, knowing that his strong-willed wife would not leave until she finished her project.

Chapter 30

Several minutes later, Annie heard someone walking down the hall, but it was way too soon for Ed to have returned. She tensed as she listened to the footsteps, then got up from her desk and called out, "Hello. Anybody here?" Heart beating fast and hearing no response, she walked to the door of her office and peered around the corner into the hallway. Then she saw him.

"Good grief, Annie, you startled me."

"Oh, it's you, Charles." Annie took a deep breath. "Didn't you hear me call out?"

Charles shook his head. "No, but my hearing's not that great, and I didn't put my hearing aids in this morning. Sorry if I scared you. What are you doing here? I didn't see any cars in the parking lot so didn't think anyone would be in the building."

"Ed dropped me off. He had to run something over to the police station but will come back for me once he's finished there. I decided to take the morning to go through some archived materials I found in boxes in the basement to see what's salvageable and what can be tossed. What are you doing here?" asked Annie.

"My doctor wants me to take a brisk walk every day; says it'll be good for my heart and for the Parkinson's. Since I'll be leaving to go back to Canada in several months, I thought I'd walk over here and start organizing my files for the next president."

Wearing baggy old tan corduroy pants, scuffed brown leather hiking boots and a red plaid shirt under a green down vest, Charles looked more like an old prospector than a retired professor. Amused, Annie observed that the slightly rumpled look was very out of character for him.

"How are you feeling?" She noticed the more defined tremor in his hands, pale face and dark shadows under his eyes.

"I've good and bad days, Annie, but I'm not going to sit around and mope. I have lots of things to take care of before I go back to Canada."

"I've something to show you."

She pulled the map out of her sweatshirt and was just starting to hand it to him when Ed walked through the door into her office and asked, "Annie, why is the front door unlocked? Oh, hello, Charles."

"The door *was* locked, Ed," replied Charles sheepishly. "I came in to do some work and used the keypad to let myself in, but I've been so preoccupied lately, I guess I forgot to lock the door behind me. As I mentioned to Annie, I didn't see any cars in the lot. I figured I'd be here by myself."

"I was just starting to show Charles the map, Ed," she said as she handed it to Charles.

"Do you think this could be a copy of a real map?" she asked.

Charles glanced at the map, and as he started to examine it, his already pale face became bone white, and his hands shook so hard that he dropped it. "Sorry. I'm having a bad spell."

Ed quickly pulled a straight-backed wooden chair from a corner of the office and Charles sat down in it, breathing rapidly, while Annie picked up the map. After a couple of minutes, his breath slowed. He held out his hand for the map and Annie handed it to him. He nodded and then clearing his throat and, pursing his lips, stared at the map.

"Why do you want me to do research on this, Annie? It looks like a crude drawing done by someone with an overactive imagination. I can't imagine it has any historical significance."

"That's just what Ed thought, too, Charles," replied Annie, "but I'm not so sure. It's dated at the bottom, and the writing looks ancient, like the original was drawn with a quill pen. The rendering of the shoreline seems like it could be an accurate representation of Lighthouse Cove back in the late 18th century. If there's even a remote possibility that this is a copy of a real one, I'd be remiss in not asking you to research it for me."

"Annie, if it's that important to you, I'll take it home and see what I can find. I have a couple of colleagues I can call who would be happy to help. But even if it is a copy of an old map, without knowing where the real one is or who created it and why, this one isn't going to have much value."

A bit disheartened, Annie argued, "But if it *is* a copy of an authentic map, we wouldn't *need* the real one. We can use this one to see if there's anything buried on the property where the X is marked. And if the original is also somewhere on the premises, we could display it with the other artifacts here. It would be a great tourist draw."

Charles' hands started shaking again and his breathing again became rapid and shallow.

"I'm not feeling very well right now, Annie. These spells come on very quickly, so I think I'll grab a couple of files and go home and look more closely at this when I get there. I can come back some other day when I'm feeling better to finish up my work here. I'll get back to you, but don't get your hopes up," Charles admonished.

"I don't need to stay with Annie while she goes through the boxes, Charles. Would you like me to drive you home?" asked Ed.

"I got here on my own power, and I can also get home on it. I don't need you to drive me," Charles responded testily, then remembering his manners, thanked Ed. "I appreciate the offer, but it's only a few blocks, and there are benches along the way if I need to stop. I'll be fine."

He turned to Annie. "I'll call you as soon as I have any information about this map."

As Charles walked down the hall to the entrance, Annie commented, "This is so sad. Charles' health seems to be worsening, and I wonder if he'll actually be well enough to make the move back to Canada."

Ed shrugged his shoulders and said, "He really should have let me drive him home. Still, you've got to respect him. He's doing the best he can to stay active and remain independent for as long as possible."

After Charles left the building, Ed told Annie about his visit to the police station. Ben had reluctantly agreed to have the coal scuttle examined to see if Emily's DNA was on it and if the splinters from her skull were from the scuttle, but he said he still believed the case had gone cold.

"We agreed that unless we find Emily's DNA on the scuttle, there's no way we'll be able to prove that that's what fractured her skull. Ben said he'll also have the lab check again for fingerprints, but as you and I discussed earlier, if we find some it won't necessarily implicate anyone because lots of people, including those who've served on the board, could have handled it at some point. We still aren't positive she actually was killed in the museum, but it's worth a shot, just in case something turns up."

He continued, "There's also the possibility the murderer may have hit her with something he was carrying with him instead of the scuttle, and Ben's also skeptical that the boxes or map have anything to do with her death. He reiterated he can't pay me, but I told him my bringing a coal scuttle to his office hardly constitutes my serving as consultant and that I'd be happy to continue to work on the case pro bono if he reopens it."

"How did he respond?"

"He's open to it but said he just can't dedicate any more police time to the case unless there's some tangible reason to do so. He was a bit curt with me, which isn't typical of him. He's usually pretty affable."

"He could just be tired, Ed. He and his family have been through a lot."

"You're probably right. He's been different since he got back from Arizona, so maybe his father-in-law's death hit him harder than we thought. I know he was close to him, plus he told me Ellen's not dealing well with it and is having trouble sleeping, which of course means that Ben's probably not getting much sleep either."

"Sounds like he's pretty stressed." Annie paused for a beat. "What are you going to do about it?"

"You mean about the case, not Ben?" Annie nodded.

"There's nothing much I can do until we find out what the results of the testing on the scuttle are. If the lab finds anything to tie it to Emily's murder, I've made up my mind that I'll press the issue with Ben to continue the investigation on my own without pay. We owe Emily and her family that much. I'll fill Carrie in about my plans, but I don't want to create a problem for her, especially since she's been ordered away from the case."

"Keeping her informed is different than getting her involved, Ed. If you uncover anything, you may need her support."

Ed nodded and, picking up a seasonal tourist magazine in the lobby, folded his body into an oversized chair in Annie's office and read it as she rummaged through the hodgepodge of boxes.

As she'd expected, most of what she found would be trashed or donated to the Salvation Army. She decided to keep and display some interesting photos, many dating back to the early 1900s.

After about half-an-hour, Annie told Ed she'd done enough for the day and would work on some of the others at another time. She locked up and the couple walked to their SUV. Ed went around to the passenger door to let Annie in and then asked her if she noticed anything unusual about Charles' reaction to the map.

"What on earth are you talking about?"

"I don't think his spell, as he called it, was the result of his illness. I think something about the map shook him up. He seemed nervous and talked about your finding it in the basement. How did he know that? You never said anything about finding it in the basement."

Annie sighed. "If Charles said he was having a spell, Ed, he was having a spell. All you had to do was look at him to see that. He's clearly not well. And he did know what I was doing since I told him before you got back from the station. It's no secret that boxes were stored down there. All board members are encouraged to explore the building, from attic to basement, when they start their terms."

She took a deep breath and continued, "Shortly after he joined the board, Charles stopped by and said he wanted to walk through the building. I was in the middle of something and asked him if he could give me a few minutes to finish up, and then I'd take him on a tour. In his own inimitable way, he said he didn't need me to act as tour guide. I know he went down to the basement because I saw him open the cellar door. When he came back up he didn't say anything about the boxes being on the floor, although he may not have gone into the back room, or if he did, he may not have thought anything about it."

Pausing for a second, she said, "You aren't thinking he could have something to do with Emily's murder? I know how your mind works. There's no way, given his condition, that he would have had the strength to kill her, drag her across the yard and throw her over the bluff. Ed, he liked her. Why would he want to kill her?"

"I have no idea. Everyone's a suspect, Annie, at least everyone without a good alibi. All we have is Charles' version of the events that morning, but we really don't know if he was telling the truth."

Exasperated, Annie replied, "You can't find a boogie man around every corner, Ed. Admit it. The case is cold, and Emily's killer probably never will be found. I think you're grasping at straws."

Silent, Ed got into the car, turned on the engine and drove home, lost in a myriad of thoughts, passing Charles who was sitting on a park bench staring into space.

*****

Shaky and short of breath, Charles realized as he saw Ed and Annie drive past him that he should have accepted their offer of a ride, but his stubbornness had gotten in the way of his making a reasoned decision. Plus, he didn't want to have to make small talk. He had a lot on his mind, and it was more productive for him to be alone as much as possible with his thoughts and plans.

After a very slow journey with lots of stops along the way, he arrived at his house, opened the door and before taking off his jacket pulled the map out of his pocket and placed it on the small side table that sat in the foyer just inside the front door. Within minutes, he had hung up his coat and started a fire in the fireplace. He picked up the map, stared at it for a couple of minutes; then made a phone call. After about half-an-hour he ended the call, shook his head, sighed, looked at the map once more, then ripped it to shreds and threw it into the fire.

Chapter 31

Ed, deep in thought, and Annie, annoyed with him, sat quietly over drinks and dinner that night. She had fixed shrimp with tomatoes and sheep's milk feta cheese, served the dish with a mixed green salad, and poured into their wine glasses the remainder of a bottle of an Italian-style red wine she'd purchased a few days earlier at a local winery. They rarely quarreled, but Annie could barely contain her anger at Ed concerning his suspicion of Charles.

"You've got to let this go, Ed. I know you're desperate to find Emily's killer. We all want that. Focusing on Charles as a suspect is ludicrous. His alibi is not only plausible, but most likely completely truthful. You saw how distraught he was the morning Emily was killed."

"I did, but I could have interpreted his reaction that morning incorrectly. He could have been distraught because he'd committed the murder, felt remorse about it, and then to cover it up told us that he'd entered the building after it happened. I've been doing this for a very long time, Annie, and something seems off about his reaction to the map."

Annie shook her head. "He's way too frail to have killed Emily, plus there's no motive. He's well-off financially from what I can gather and retired from a long, stellar career. What could he want in the museum? If he suspected there's something of historical significance hidden here, all he had to do was ask me for help. I know he would have."

The phone rang as Ed started to reply. He walked over to it and picked up the receiver. "Hello? Oh, hi, Charles. No, you weren't disturbing our dinner. We're almost finished. Do you want me to put Annie on? Oh. I'll tell her, but she'll be disappointed. Are you feeling any better? Good to hear. Take care of yourself. Thanks for the call."

Annie looked quizzically at Ed, her eyebrows raised. "I'm glad you were able to be cordial to Charles, despite your suspicions. I'm assuming the map has no value?"

"Charles says the map is completely bogus. The cartography shows an incorrect rendering of the shoreline for Lighthouse Cove, even for a couple of centuries ago, and he's pretty sure the writing came from a thin line indelible marker."

"Well, that's disappointing. I had hoped it was a copy of a real treasure map."

"I know you did, and after thinking about it awhile, I think you may be right. I believe Charles could be lying, and there's a connection between that map and Emily's death. As I was beginning to say before he called, although he's in ill health and despite his frailness, Emily was so tiny that he might have had the strength to drag her body to the bluff and roll it over, especially if he had an adrenalin rush after assuming he'd killed her. We didn't see signs of dragging because the snow started falling after she was killed. There already was a thick covering on the ground before Ben arrived at the scene."

"Ed, there's no way that Charles would be involved in Emily's murder. I'm positive of that, and I can't imagine there's even a remote connection between the map and what happened to her. While I'd love for it to be authentic, Ed, if Charles says the map's not a copy of a real one, I believe him. I think you're grasping at straws because you don't have any other suspects and can't find a motive."

"Can we let this go for now, Annie? We have a difference of opinion, and until I have more information, there's no sense arguing about it. But please don't go back into the basement until we get this cleared up."

Annie sighed. "Yes, we can let this go for now, and I won't go back into the basement until you or Carrie tell me it's okay. But I hope this is one time you're wrong."

Chapter 32

Unable to stop obsessing about the case, Ed tossed and turned for most of the night and finally got out of bed at 5:30 a.m. He made a pot of coffee, and after pouring himself a large mug went into his study where he sat in his leather recliner and mulled over the details of the investigation. He believed that if not Emily's killer, Charles knew something about who was. Annie found him still sitting there at 7 a.m.

"Bad night? You were pretty restless."

"Sorry. I hope I didn't keep you awake."

"I was able to get some sleep, despite your tossing and turning. What's bothering you that you couldn't sleep?"

"I spent most of the night thinking about our conversation with Charles and his reaction when you handed him the map. I think it's a copy of a real one, and he knows it. I'm positive it's tied to Emily's murder. If he's not the killer, he's shielding someone. I'm going to call Ben and get his permission to go to Charles' house later this morning and talk with him."

Annie shook her head and walked out of the study without responding.

Ben wasn't in his office when Ed called, so he asked to speak with Carrie. He summarized the events of the previous day and told her he wanted to interview Charles.

"I can't imagine Ben would have any problem with your doing that, Ed, as long as you understand that we can't pay you. As deputy chief, I'm going to give you the go ahead to talk with him. Poor Ben. He got a call from his father last night. His mother had a stroke. He and Ellen are now on their way to Wisconsin. They can't seem to get a break. He's not sure how long he'll be gone, but I'll fill him in when he gets back."

Charles' doorbell rang at 10 a.m. He looked out the large bay window in his living room and saw Ed standing in the covered entrance at the end of the brick path that led to his house from the street. He was tempted to not go to the door, certain that the purpose of the visit was to continue the discussion about the map, something he didn't want to waste any more time on. But he also knew that if he didn't respond he'd have to talk with Ed some other day, so he might as well get this over with.

Built on land that was subdivided during the 1970s as part of an estate settlement of a ship's captain's mansion built in the late 19th century, the pale yellow-sided one-story ranch-style home had white trim, slate-colored architectural shingles on the mansard roof, an integral one-car garage and a small yard with a clutch of evergreens, azaleas and rhododendrons clustered along the front of the house.

Taking a deep breath, Charles opened his white paneled front door. "Good morning, Ed. Is there something I can help you with?"

"I'd like to ask you some more questions, Charles, about the day of Emily's murder." responded Ed.

Surprised, Charles opened the door, motioned for Ed to enter and pointed to the pale beige upholstered sofa with blue and beige plaid accent pillows that was sitting against the wall opposite the front window. "Please have a seat," he said, and then slid into one of two blue and beige plaid upholstered chairs that faced the sofa.

At the far end of one side of the room, wood logs burned in the fireplace. Ed noticed an arrangement of photos displayed on the mantel above it, and before sitting, he walked over to look at them. One was with Charles, what appeared to be some of his university colleagues, and a younger man, probably a student, in a large office. Another was a photo of Charles, seeming to be in his 50s, and two other men grinning and displaying three very large steelhead trout; yet another portrayed a much younger and very debonair Charles, with his arm around a striking young woman in front of what looked like the Tower of London in England.

"Nice photos," Ed remarked. "Who's the pretty woman?"

Charles told him he'd had a relationship with her when he was in graduate school, but the relationship had ended. Ed thought it odd that he still displayed the photo but decided it wouldn't be appropriate to pry.

Charles asked, "Why are you here, Ed? What do you want?"

"Why did you retire to Lighthouse Cove, Charles?" queried Ed.

"Excuse me? I don't understand why that's at all pertinent to your investigation of Emily's murder."

"Humor me, Charles. The question *is* related to the investigation. I'm curious about why you ended up here instead of staying in Canada. Wouldn't that have made more sense for you than retiring to the states?"

Charles rolled his eyes and sighed. "I have dual citizenship. My mother was born here, so while my permanent residence was in Canada, it was very easy for me to relocate to the states. I passed through here several years ago with some colleagues on our way to the Finger Lakes and fell in love with it. Most of the small towns and villages along Lake Ontario in Canada, while quaint and charming, don't have the rugged coastal beauty of this village, and it seemed like the perfect place for me to retire."

"Then I'll get to the point. I think you are lying about that map. I think it may be a copy of a real one, and you know something about it. I think it's tied to Emily's murder. May I see it, please?"

This does have something to do with the map, Charles thought, irritated that he had to be addressing the issue yet again.

"You're wrong. It's nothing, believe me, I tossed it," Charles sputtered. "It's of absolutely no value to the historical society. The copy could only exist if there's a real one somewhere and if that's the case, why hasn't that one surfaced? Without it, there's absolutely no way to prove that this is a copy of an authentic one."

"Charles, you're not making any sense. There could be a number of reasons why the original, if there is one, hasn't surfaced. I believe you know something about this map and that it's related to the real reason Emily was killed. I think you're withholding information, but I don't understand why. You cared for Emily, why wouldn't you want us to find her killer unless somehow you were involved?"

"You're accusing me of killing Emily? That's preposterous! Do I need to call an attorney?"

"I'm not accusing you, but I think you know something about her death. You don't need to call an attorney, but please don't leave town. I may be back to you with more questions."

Ed's cell phone rang. He saw it was a call from Carrie. "I need to take this. Remember what I just told you," he admonished.

Ed walked outside and answered the phone. "Yeah. I'm not surprised that Emily's DNA was found on the scuttle. The epithelial cells from her scalp matched, didn't they? Did the lab find any prints? That's too bad. I'd hoped that some of them would be on file. Maybe the killer was wearing gloves, which is why he didn't feel the need to get rid of the scuttle after he used it to strike her. At least we know we have our murder weapon. I'll get back to you after I finish talking with Charles."

"One more thing, Ed, before you hang up," Carrie said. "The crime lab also gave me the report on the chain that Annie found. They couldn't find anything to tie it to Emily's murder."

"That's disappointing, Carrie. So even though we know that Emily was hit with the scuttle, we're really not any further along in finding out who murdered her."

Chapter 33

While Ed was questioning Charles, Annie took a
long brisk walk to work off her anger at him. An inch
of newly fallen snow, as white as a starched tuxedo
shirt, lay on the grass, a sharp contrast to the wet, black
macadam roads. White caps on a thick-as-sludge steel
blue sea punched onto the beach, layer upon layer, and
froze, creating a stunning winter tableau of miniature,
translucent icebergs. She arrived home at the same time
as Ed.

"Well? Is he your murderer?" she asked icily.

Ed sighed. "I'm positive he knows something,
Annie, despite what you think. Either he killed Emily or
is shielding the person who did. I asked him to give the
map back to me, but he said he got rid of it. If it had no
value, he still could have offered to return it to you to
use in whatever way you saw fit rather than destroying
it. I'm sorry we didn't make a copy; it was stupid of me
to not think about doing that."

Annie stared at Ed for a moment and then smiled
smugly before speaking. "I don't believe for a second
that Charles had anything to do with Emily's murder,
but I figured even if Charles said it wasn't a copy of a
real one, I could still have some fun using it at a
children's treasure hunt, so I made a copy. I was
concerned that, given how shaky he is, Charles would
spill something on it or damage it after I gave it to him.
It's in the desk in my office."

"You're terrific, do you know that?"

"I'm glad you appreciate me." Annie grinned.

"I'm sorry we're at odds about this, Annie. We've been married long enough for you to know by now that my instincts are usually spot on. I truly believe Charles knows or is hiding something about the murder."

"I guess my emotions are getting the better of me, Ed," Annie admitted. "I simply can't believe Charles would have anything to do with Emily's murder, but I also do know you well enough to know that you're rarely wrong when it comes to putting pieces together to solve a crime."

"Thanks," Ed said, and hugged his wife. "I do understand how upset you are and that you're having trouble believing Charles might be involved. Let me make it up to you. How would you like to go to Toronto with me tomorrow? I spoke with Carrie after I finished interviewing Charles and when I told her what I suspected, she agreed that I should make a trip there. We could come back tomorrow evening or spend the night."

"Do you think there's something in Canada that's related to Emily's murder?"

"I have a hunch that there may be a link to the map and her murder with the department where Charles taught at the University of Toronto. He knows much more than he's telling us. I'm going to take the map with me and talk with the dean of the department of archaeology to see if I can learn a little more about the projects he was involved with before he retired."

"We haven't been to Toronto in ages, and I'd love to go. If I can get Sandy to keep Gretchen on such short notice, instead of doing a day trip, let's spend the night. We have an almost three-hour drive each way, and it'll give us some time together during the drive and once you're finished at the university, Yorkville has some nice hotels and is just a stone's throw from the university's main campus.

"You could drop me off there while you go visit the dean. I can do some shopping, have lunch, visit a gallery or two and then maybe we could have dinner tomorrow night at an intimate bistro. I get tired of wearing jeans and sweaters all the time, and it would be nice to dress up a bit and eat gourmet food for a change."

Chapter 34

The scenic route to Canada, Route 104, meandered along Lake Ontario skirting stands of sea grasses, desolate beaches and lakeside picnicking sites. Wintering snow geese huddled together among the marshes, with an occasional family of white swans gliding through wetlands and pools of rippling, sun-dappled water that lapped onto the shore.

At the end of the route in western New York, the Lewiston-Queenston Bridge spanned the Niagara River Gorge, intersecting on the Canadian side with the Queen Elizabeth Way, or QEW, that led directly into the bustling city of Toronto. The fourth largest city in North America, it boasted a skyline along the lake that rivaled that of Manhattan's, the CN tower prominent as tourists drove into the downtown.

The night before, after Annie confirmed with their pet sitter that she could look after Gretchen, Ed called and made a reservation at a boutique hotel on Bloor Street, right in the heart of Yorkville, a trendy now upscale part of town that in the 1960s had attracted long-haired university students wearing bell bottoms, tie-dyed shirts and beads, and carrying peace signs.

Ed dropped Annie and their overnight bags off at the entrance to the hotel, summoned a bellhop to help her with the bags and to check-in, and then headed to the main campus of the university for his meeting with the dean of the archaeology department.

After being announced by her assistant, Jerome, a slightly built young Asian man who sat behind a large, oak desk outside her office, a petite woman in her 40s with golden brown skin, almond-shaped brown eyes and curly thick brown hair parted on one side and falling to her chin greeted him and introduced herself as Jennifer Ashwani. She wore a tailored blazer, knee-length straight skirt and high leather boots. Her jewelry consisted of a wide gold wedding band, gold studs in her ears and a watch with a small oval face and slim gold strap. She stuck out her hand, and Ed took it, thanking her for seeing him on such short notice.

"What can I do for you, Chief DeCleryk?"

"Please, Dean Ashwani, call me Ed."

She smiled. "Then let's drop the formality on both sides. Please call me Jennifer. Why don't you come into my office, and we can talk?" She motioned him to proceed before her into her office.

Against the far wall between two tall, narrow windows, a sturdy mahogany desk with an upholstered chair faced into the room towards the door. Along the left side of the room, a leather loveseat and two small wing chairs were grouped around a small oval mahogany coffee table. A bookcase filled with professional journals had been placed against the opposite wall, fronted by a round table with four upholstered bucket-shaped chairs clustered around it.

"Okay if I sit there?" Ed pointed at the loveseat.

"Of course," replied the dean, taking one of the chairs across from him. She gestured towards a silver beverage set placed on the coffee table next to a plate of biscuits. "Can I offer you some tea or coffee? These lemon biscuits are quite tasty."

Ed accepted a cup of tea and a biscuit, and after several quiet seconds of sipping and munching, he pulled the map out of his pocket.

"Do you recognize this, Jennifer?"

"Of course, I recognize it. It's a copy of the framed original that's kept in a small climate-controlled exhibit space containing artifacts from archaeological digs. I can show it to you before you leave. Where did you find it?"

"That's what I thought, and I'm not surprised. We found it in the basement of the historical society museum in Lighthouse Cove, NY. We think it's related to a murder we're trying to solve that occurred there."

"A murder? That's terrible. What would this map have to do with a murder?"

"It's a long story, and we're still trying to put the pieces together. But before I tell you more, if you wouldn't mind, could you describe the circumstances surrounding the discovery of the map?"

"Of course." She proceeded to tell Ed about a law in Ontario that requires any new residential or commercial development to be preceded by a dig on the site.

She said, "Artifacts dating back centuries kept on turning up during the building boom that occurred here during the last couple of decades, and the planning commission, wanting to make sure that our history is preserved as much as possible, got the law passed.

"It happened before I started working here, but from my understanding, archaeologists found the map during a dig that took place prior to development of a new upscale condo complex. The land in question was part of a settlement of traders who lived there starting in the late 1700s, when Toronto was known as York and was part of Canada, British North America. The neighborhood, located north of the downtown, was in the process of being gentrified, and the developers had already torn down a couple of rows of factory homes built in the 1930s that had no real historic value. Underneath those, the team of archaeologists unearthed remnants of log cabins and a treasure trove of artifacts dating back to that time."

"Interesting. Did they find anything valuable?"

"Among the normal things like pieces of broken cookware, tools, weapons and bits of clothing, they unearthed a copper box, somewhat rusted, but still remarkably preserved, that they found among the rubble of a stone fireplace. In it were a handwritten map and a manuscript written by a man named Thomas Battleforth. The old-fashioned, spidery penmanship made it hard to read, but some of our staff are pretty adept at deciphering old handwriting."

She continued, "Battleforth tells an incredible story, not only about his life, but also about valuable treasure belonging to British royalty that historians had always assumed was lost when a British ship, the HMS Orion, capsized in a storm on Lake Ontario in the late 1700s."

"I know about that ship," Ed interjected. "My wife is the executive director of the historical society, and she mentions it in a history she just wrote about Lighthouse Cove. A son and daughter-in-law of the King of England went down with the ship, and there were rumors that treasure was lost at sea. Divers discovered some remains, but the treasure was never found."

"That's correct," replied Jennifer. "But the treasure may not have gone down with ship, as you'll read in the manuscript. Even so, the historical significance of the manuscript and the map were important enough for us to decide to display them in our archive room, along with the rusted box. Because the paper was so dry and brittle, we couldn't copy it, so we had it typed up, published and offer that version for sale in our bookstore. I can give you my copy if you'd like. For many reasons, I think you'll find it fascinating."

She walked over to a bookshelf, pulled out a slim, perfect-bound book and handed it to him. "I don't need it back. I can get another. It should take you an hour or less to read."

She paused for a second. "Let me ask you something, if you don't mind."

"Of course," Ed replied.

"Your last name is an unusual one. Is there any possibility your ancestors settled in Lighthouse Cove?"

"Yes, right after the Revolutionary War. I was born and raised there. Why are you asking?"

"I don't want to spoil the fun by telling you, but I think you're really going to enjoy reading this," she responded, smiling, as she handed him the manuscript.

Accepting it, Ed thanked her and asked, "Do you know who led the team from the university?"

"Yes. His name is Charles Merrill, but I've not met him. I moved here three years ago from Vancouver to take this position. Charles retired before I took this job, but when you read the manuscript you'll understand why this project was so important to him."

"I know Charles," he responded. "He's living in Lighthouse Cove and president of the board of the historical society. We found a copy of the map at what appears to be the crime scene, but when we showed it to him to ask him to help us authenticate it, he argued it couldn't possibly be a facsimile of a real one. My wife asked him to check it out anyway. He took it home, promising to do some research on it just in case he was wrong, but later called and said he was standing by his original assessment and destroyed it without even asking if we wanted it back. Fortunately, my wife made a copy. Charles acted as though he'd never seen it before, which given what you've just told me, is very puzzling. Why would he do that?"

"I have no idea," responded Jennifer. "He has an excellent reputation, and from what I've heard about him, it would seem odd that he'd be involved in anything criminal. But as I said, I don't know him."

She thought for a few seconds and then continued, "You know, the former dean, Angelica Hawthorn, retired to Niagara-on-the-Lake. I heard that she and Charles were close friends, and she has far more knowledge about him and the dig than I do. If I had more time I'd be happy to call her for you and explain why you'd like to speak with her, but I have a meeting in 15 minutes. I want to show you our archive room before I go. I don't think she'd mind if I give you her phone number."

Ed thanked her and said he appreciated the lead. After adding Dr. Hawthorn's information into his cell phone contacts, he followed Jennifer down the hall to a small, climate-controlled room set up inside like an art gallery, but with cabinets with glass doors lining one wall. The original map, the rusted box and the small, tattered chamois-bound manuscript sat inside one of the cabinets. Looking at the artifacts, Ed shook his head in amazement, thanked Jennifer again and headed outside to telephone the former dean.

Chapter 35

At approximately the same time that Ed and Jennifer Ashwani were sipping their tea, Carrie was perusing a brief Ben had given to her about Homeland Security measures along shorelines located near international borders. She had just turned a page when Brad, on duty at the front desk, buzzed her phone intercom and told her that she had a visitor. She closed the brief and told him to send him back to her office. A few seconds later, she heard footsteps outside her door. She looked up, smiled, and greeted her visitor. "Hi, come on in. What can I do for you?"

*****

Ed, in the meantime, had spoken with Angelica Hawthorn, who indicated a willingness to see him at 2:30 p.m. He grabbed a quick lunch at a Tim Horton's Café and Bakeshop and then headed south towards Niagara-on-the-Lake, a charming Canadian town situated at the confluence of the Niagara River and Lake Ontario, north of Niagara Falls. Tudor-style and Victorian homes with wide expanses of lawn backed up to the river or bordered vineyards, which, like their counterparts in the Finger Lakes, had proliferated since the 1990s as increasing numbers of drinkers switched from hard liquor to wine.

Spring through late fall, buses and cars filled with eager tourists descended upon the quaint town to explore wineries, shop at British-themed boutiques and attend the Shaw Festival, a series of live theatre performances consisting of dramas, farces and comedies written by George Bernard Shaw and his contemporaries or by modern playwrights with Shavian sensibilities. The visitors lodged at inns and beds-and-breakfasts with names honoring British kings and queens, and took their meals at pubs, bistros and tea rooms named for British royalty and botanicals like willow, thistle and cabbage rose.

Dr. Hawthorn lived at the end of Ivy Street in a charming Queen Anne-style home replete with turrets, wide porches and stained-glass windows. Not finding a doorbell, Ed rapped the simple brass knocker on the door, and in a few seconds a slender, statuesque woman with piercing blue eyes and white hair styled in a chignon low against her neck answered the door. Smiling, she extended her hand.

"You must be Ed DeCleryk. I'm Angelica. Please come inside."

Ed followed her into the foyer of the grand house. She glided, rather than walked, reinforcing Ed's impression she might be one of the most serene women he'd ever met. She wore an angora turtleneck sweater, soft, flowing jersey pants, and soft leather flats. Her only jewelry was a wide platinum wedding band encrusted with a multitude of tiny pavé diamonds. She noticed him glancing at it.

"I'm usually not big on jewelry but my husband bought it for me for our 25th anniversary. Stunning, isn't it?"

"It's quite eye-catching. Tell me about him and what brought the two of you here," requested Ed, thinking a bit of small talk might help create a bond between himself and the older woman.

"He's a retired professor of theatre arts from York University. While he was still working, he'd act in a couple of plays during summer break, and now that we live here full time, he also sits on the Shaw Festival governing board. We used to live near the Botanical Garden in Toronto but moved here after we both retired because we not only love the town, but also because it's much easier for him to be involved with the Festival when he doesn't have to drive from Toronto."

"What about you? After living in a large city like Toronto this must be quite a change for you."

Angelica laughed. "Excuse the cliché, but I took to living here like a duck takes to water. We're so close to Toronto that I can easily get there when I want to, and in the meantime, we get all the benefits of living in a small community like the slower pace of life and actually knowing and being friendly with our neighbors."

"Sounds a lot like Lighthouse Cove," Ed remarked.

"It's wonderful, isn't it?" she responded.

Ed smiled and asked, "So how do *you* spend your time?"

"During warmer months, I garden and play golf. I'm also involved in the civic club and historical society, belong to a book discussion group, play bridge, take afternoon tea with friends and attend cultural events. I'm writing a book about the architectural history of this region. We live a comfortable, peaceful and extremely happy life."

After offering Ed some refreshments, which he declined, she said, "Now, how I can help you?"

Ed told her about Emily's murder, the break-in that had occurred the morning she was killed and the subsequent discovery of a copy of the map. He explained how Charles had denied knowledge of it despite Jennifer Ashwani verifying that he'd been part of a dig that had unearthed it along with Thomas Battleforth's manuscript.

"Jennifer gave me a copy of the manuscript which I obviously haven't had time to read yet, but she did tell me that it has to do with treasure that was thought to be lost at sea during the wreck of the HMS Orion in the late 1700s. I know about that; my wife is the head of our historical society and recently wrote a history of our community, but it just doesn't make sense that Charles would lie about not knowing about the map."

"You're right; it makes no sense at all"

"How well do you really know him?"

"Quite well," she responded and proceeded to tell Ed that she had met Charles while they both were attending Cambridge University in England as doctoral candidates and that they'd had an intimate relationship.

She smiled. "He was quite the catch in those days."

"You must be the gorgeous woman in the photo with Charles in front of the Tower of London," Ed exclaimed. "It's displayed on his mantel."

Angelica blushed. "Thank you. The photo was taken when we visited London during our spring break. How odd that he's kept it. While I did love him, for a number of reasons the relationship didn't work out, and we eventually went our separate ways."

Single, content and not expecting to ever marry, her plans changed when she met her husband one summer while attending a workshop in Toronto. There was instant chemistry, and they married but maintained separate residences for many years because she was teaching at McGill University in Montreal. When she learned that the University of Toronto department of archaeology was seeking a new dean she applied for and was awarded the position, having no idea at the time that Charles served on the faculty. Shortly after she was hired and just before she'd scheduled her first faculty meeting, he made an appointment to see her.

Because she continued to use her family name professionally, Charles assumed she was still single and confessed he had always hoped that they'd meet again and would be able to rekindle their romance with the possibility of making it permanent. She'd replied that she was happily married but was confident they'd be able to put the past aside and be able to work together as colleagues at the university.

"Charles was disappointed but seemed to accept there was no romantic future for us, and we were able to work amicably together for the remainder of our time at the university and actually became close friends. Some months after I joined the department, he found the map and manuscript at the dig and then, after carbon dating it for authenticity, spent quite a bit of time trying to figure out exactly where the supposed treasure was located. The drawing was crude, and the manuscript alluded to a spit of land settled after the American Revolution by Dutch and French Colonists on the southern shores of Lake Ontario in New York."

"Did you contact anyone in Great Britain about partnering with you on a dig in New York after what you found?"

"No, not at that time. We all knew that a ship carrying British royals and their valuables went down in a storm on the lake in the late 1700s, but we wanted to make sure Battleforth's story had credibility before contacting them."

"What happened next?"

"Charles arranged a meeting with his teaching assistant, a local surveyor, and a geologist on our faculty and together they determined that the shoreline around Lighthouse Cove was the most likely spot. He called the historical society there early in November, but the message on the answering machine indicated it had closed for the season. Once we got back to Toronto he called again, and this time left a message, hoping someone would retrieve it. No one returned his call— we discovered later that the director had resigned and returned to her home in England—the four decided to make an exploratory trip to Lighthouse Cove along with a student who was writing a feature article about Charles for the university newspaper.

"We had planned to approach the historical society board in Lighthouse Cove about working on a joint venture, but once they got to the site, the geologist and surveyor concluded it had been a wild goose chase. Measuring off the land from its edge to the "X" on the map where the treasure was supposedly buried would have located it directly inside the museum.

"But over the past couple of centuries or more the bluff has eroded, the coastline has dramatically shifted, and we know the original lighthouse was rebuilt and moved farther back from the bluff. They determined that the treasure, if it truly hadn't gone down with the ship, couldn't possibly be inside the building and it would be a complete exercise in futility to try and find it on the land where the museum stood or buried somewhere in the sand.

"The TA disagreed with the decision and tried to persuade the others that there was compelling scientific evidence proving that the treasure could be inside the building. Although terribly disappointed for reasons I'll tell you about in a second, Charles had the final word, trusted the others on the team and supported them."

"Might he think you or some of the others might be involved in the break-in or Emily's murder?"

"Charles knew how disappointed both Pamela and I were at not being able to move forward with the project. Finding treasure like that described in the manuscript would have been a huge coup for the University. We would have sent the artifacts back to England, of course, and as a result our department's reputation would have soared in archaeological circles. Still, it would be a stretch to think that Charles would lie about the map or cover for one of us because he believed we had decided to go back to Lighthouse Cove to try and find the treasure on our own."

She continued, "Charles knows as well as I do that doing even a simple excavation would require certain professional tools that aren't terribly easy to cart around. Perhaps the simplest answer to why Charles got shaky when your wife handed him the map is that he didn't expect to see it there and was shocked and surprised but for reasons unbeknown to us, decided to not say anything about it until he thought a bit more about why it might have been there in the first place."

"Charles is having some health problems, Angelica. He may not have been thinking rationally." He told her about Charles' heart condition and Parkinson's disease and his decision to move back to Toronto.

"I'm so sorry to hear that. I must reach out to him and let him know that Miles and I are here for him, once he moves back to Canada. Now that I know Charles is ill there's another possibility, and this may make more sense. It may have something to do with his wanting to right a wrong he believes was done by his family centuries ago.

"It's complicated, but once you read Battleforth's manuscript you'll understand. What doesn't make sense is why he wouldn't have gone to the historical society board to let them know he suspected the treasure might be buried underneath the museum, unless he was afraid they wouldn't believe him or if they did and an excavation didn't pan out that he'd lose face."

"Angelica, is it remotely possible he could have decided to go into the museum at night or early in the morning when others weren't around, just to do some exploring to make sure he could build a case for doing some sort of excavation before going to the board?"

"Perhaps, but it's a bit of a stretch to imagine. Maybe Charles did go to the museum early in the morning of the murder and either found your victim already dead or may have been involved in what was possibly a very tragic accident. In that case, though, even with his illness and the possibility he might not have been thinking clearly, it's inconceivable to me that he wouldn't have called for help."

Ed asked, "I know about the treasure being lost, but can you tell me what type of treasure we're talking about?"

"Please read the manuscript, it's quite fascinating and will give you some of the answers you seek, but I can tell you that Battleforth claims that he, at one time, was in possession of jewelry and other valuables that he'd stolen from the British royal family and buried somewhere within the vicinity of the land your museum in Lighthouse Cove stands on. If that's true, then today it would be worth millions of dollars.

"Why isn't this common knowledge?"

"We were able to find written records indicating that the royals made the journey with valuables, but no records exist listing what they were. After making the trip to Lighthouse Cove, we decided we simply didn't have enough proof that they were buried somewhere within the vicinity of your museum to contact officials in England."

"Given what you've told me, I'm becoming certain that Charles may have been involved in Emily's death or be covering for someone who was responsible. If the latter is true, then I must ask you this as a formality, can you tell me where you were the night of the murder?"

"I know you do. Miles and I were at a fund-raising gala for the Shaw Festival that night. I'll give you the name of the board president and some others who were there if you like."

"What about the others on the team? Could any of them have changed their mind and gone to Lighthouse Cove to do some exploring?"

"I doubt it. The geologist, Kate Chu, moved away and is now living in British Columbia. I believe that Barry Eaton, the surveyor, still works for the planning commission in Toronto. But remember, they were the ones who cautioned against pursuing the matter any further, believing it would be an exercise in futility. I doubt they've changed their minds.

"The teaching assistant, Pamela Huntsman, is now an associate professor in our department. I can give you her phone number and email address. She's married with young children, and while she's ambitious, she's also quite steady. Since she was with the group who traveled to Lighthouse Cove, she may have some insights about the trip that I don't.

"I can't remember the student's name, and while he wanted to see us pursue the dig, my sense was that it was only because it would make a great feature story for the newspaper. I don't think he was all that invested otherwise, and he wasn't present during the discussion when we determined to not move ahead with the project. Pam may remember who he was and might be able to get you his contact information as well as the others if you want to try and contact them."

Angelica wrote Pamela's phone number on a small piece of paper and gave it to Ed. "Here's her number. I don't think she'd mind you calling her. I just can't believe any of the team would break into your museum in the dead of night to try and locate treasure that most likely was never there in the first place. How the map got there may always remain a mystery."

Ed glanced at his watch. It was getting late, and he had at least an hour's drive back to Toronto.

He rose and said, "I need to get going. My wife came with me on this trip and is shopping and sightseeing in Yorkville. I've promised the evening to her and want to make sure I get back in time to change before dinner. Thank you so much for your help. You've filled in some blanks for me, and I have a lot to think about."

They clasped hands. "Please call me anytime, Ed, especially if you have questions after you read the manuscript."

Chapter 36

Ed called Annie. "Hi, honey. I'm in Niagara-on-the-Lake but getting ready to head back to Toronto. Long story, which I will tell you about tonight at dinner. Were you able to make a dinner reservation somewhere?"

"I was, but not until 8:00 and the restaurant, Au Jour Le Jour, is only a few doors down from the hotel, so take your time. We're in room 403. There's a key waiting for you at the front desk. I have a few more things I want to do, so I'll see you later."

On his way out the door, he heard the chiming of an incoming text message. It was from Carrie. "Call me. It's important."

"Hmm. Wonder if something's broken with the case." He phoned Carrie.

"Hi, Carrie. It's Ed. What's up?"

"We may have closed the case, Ed. Charles came in to see me a little while ago and confessed to killing Emily."

Ed shook his head and responded, "I don't believe it. I should be very pleased about his confession, Carrie, since I was the one who thought all along that he most likely was Emily's murderer. Now I'm not so sure. I just finished interviewing the current and former deans of his department at the university, and after talking with them it seems more and more plausible that he may be covering for someone else. What did he tell you?"

"He admitted he lied about the map. Like we thought, it's a copy of a real one that's displayed among other historical documents at the University of Toronto, and the one Annie showed him was his. He said he had two copies of the original, one he kept at home and one in the false bottom of a drawer in the antique desk in Emily's office. He knew about the drawer because she'd shown it to him."

"Why would he keep a copy of it in the museum? That doesn't make sense. Why not in a safe deposit box?"

Carrie answered, "I asked him why he hadn't kept it in a safe deposit box. He said he didn't think he needed to because he had two copies and could always get another from the university, but he didn't want to keep them at home for some reason."

"This is sounding a bit far-fetched, don't you think? What happened next?"

"He started having second thoughts about his decision to not go ahead with the excavation. He'd taken out the copy he kept at home to look at again but, because of the Parkinson's, spilled coffee on it.

"He hadn't been sleeping well so went into the museum around 6:00 on the morning Emily was murdered to get the copy hidden in the desk because he didn't want to have to explain why it was there in the first place. He'd planned to approach Annie to see about the possibility of doing an archaeological excavation. He said his purpose would have been to get the treasure back to its rightful owner. I asked him what he meant about that, and he mumbled something about his family being responsible for its disappearance. Do you know what he's talking about?"

Ed told her about the manuscript and the authentic map plus what he had learned about the treasure.

"Angelica Hawthorn indicated that Charles may have wanted to right a wrong done by one of his ancestors, I'm assuming that person was this man, Battleforth. She said the story was complicated, so I'd have to read the manuscript to get the answers we need, but I haven't had time yet. Did he tell you what happened with Emily?"

"He did. He said he heard her come in while he was going through the desk, and scared that it was an intruder went into the basement to hide. He had just enough time to grab the map and close the desk drawer. He said he saw someone come down the cellar steps with a lighted flashlight in hand but didn't recognize Emily until she got closer.

"It was very dark in the basement, and when Emily saw Charles she screamed, not recognizing him, then tripped and fell. She got up, bruised and scared, and ran towards the steps. He said he called out to her and identified himself, but she was so terrified that he thinks she didn't hear him and ran up the steps to get away. He followed her, identifying himself again, but when he reached for her, she pushed him away, he grabbed for her and she fell again, hitting her head against the radiator in her office and losing consciousness.

"He said he tried to revive her, but she didn't gain consciousness, and thinking she was dead he panicked. Dragging her body to the bluff, he threw it over, forgetting about her coat and purse. He said he wasn't in his right mind. He reminded me that he's been ill and that both the heart condition and the Parkinson's have been affecting him emotionally, plus mental confusion and paranoia can be side effects of one of the meds he's on. He admitted he knew he should have called 911. When he got back to the museum to clean up, he saw her coat and purse and staged what looked like an attempted burglary to get the police off track."

"He knows enough about what happened to Emily that he could have put some of the other pieces together to come up with a plausible story," Ed remarked. "Did he offer any information about the map and why it was placed between the two boxes?"

"He said he had dropped the map in the struggle and when it didn't show up when Annie cleaned up after the bogus burglary he thought it had been destroyed or tossed. He didn't know what had happened to it until he learned, some weeks later, that Annie discovered it when you and she went to down to the basement the day she showed it to him. He denied putting it there.

"He admitted he lied to you and Annie that day because it would have implicated him in Emily's murder and that he was in shock and denial over what he had done. He rationalized that her death wasn't his fault but the result of a tragic accident. Since then his conscience hasn't stopped bothering him, causing sleeplessness and worsening his health, thus the confession."

"I suppose if the cellar door were open the map could have landed in the basement," replied Ed. "What I don't understand is why we found it between the two boxes. Is there any possibility that Luke or one of the forensic technologists found it and not thinking it was related to the crime but assuming it might be something that Annie might need, put it between the boxes for safe keeping?"

"I asked them. No one remembers doing anything like that, but in fairness they said the building was such a mess that one of them could easily have put it there without thinking. Still, that no one remembers is kind of odd."

"What about the hole in the floor in the basement?"

"When questioned, Charles said he didn't know anything about it, and seemed truly puzzled. I believe him. I suppose our initial premise could be correct that some workers had dug up old pipes and put the boxes over the hole until they could come back to finish the job but never did and that someone else saw the hole and covered it."

"Something else confuses me about his confession, Carrie," remarked Ed. "The crime lab reported that the coal scuttle had DNA from Emily's scalp, which made us sure it was the murder weapon. Charles didn't say what Emily fell against in the basement, and it very well may have been the scuttle, but when someone trips they usually fall forward, and we know for sure her injuries were on the back of the head. I can't remember the report indicating lacerations or dirt on her face from a fall forward or reading anything about evidence being found on the radiator."

"She did have dirt on her face, Ed, and lacerations that we assumed were the result of being thrown over the bluff. But you're right, there was no mention of the radiator. I guess it is possible Emily walked into something in the basement, like a low hanging pipe, lost her balance and fell backward, hitting her head against the scuttle but she didn't lose consciousness," Carrie surmised.

"It's also possible Charles only thought her head hit the radiator, but it didn't, which would explain why the techs found strands of Emily's hair on the floor in her office. His eyesight isn't good, and there was almost no light in the basement and only a small low-watt lamp on her desk, so he could have been confused. It's doubtful that tripping and falling in the basement or falling against the radiator would have resulted in a skull fracture, unless she took an especially hard blow."

"And you're sure they checked the radiator?"

"Yes. There was absolutely no mention in their report of hair or cells on the radiator," replied Carrie.

"Carrie, despite Charles' confession, my instincts are telling me he wasn't completely truthful with you. I'm starting to believe he may be covering for someone.

"Emily's reaction and Charles' response just doesn't seem in character for either of them. Yes, she would have been scared, but as soon as she recognized Charles or heard him call out to her, she would have calmed down, even given her heightened sense of alertness based on what we know of her state of mind at that time."

"I agree with you, Ed. I truly believe Charles would have done everything he could to save Emily. He seems like a responsible man and, once Emily went down, he would have called 911. We would have viewed what happened as an accident, and by calling us he may have been able to save her life. Unfortunately, we have no other suspects so unless someone else comes forward to confess to the murder we may have no choice but to consider the case closed."

"Where's Charles now, Carrie?"

"He's in custody. We read him his rights, but he waived them. He said he was ready to tell us what happened and didn't need an attorney to be present. After he wrote and signed the confession, we arrested him, filed the complaint, and he's now sitting in a cell waiting to be arraigned. He told me he intends to plead guilty to avoid the case going to a grand jury and to avoid a trial, although once he retains legal counsel that person may get him to change his mind. He's scheduled to appear before the judge tomorrow, and since he's already agreed to surrender his passport we won't oppose bail, but I wish there were a way to release him tonight. But that's not going to happen unless someone else confesses pretty quickly."

She changed the subject. "How are things going there?"

"It's been a long and very interesting day. I'll give you the full details when I see you tomorrow. I should be pleased at Charles' confession, but there's also a possibility he's protecting the real killer because he's already in ill health and willing to take the fall for that person. What I'd like to do, if you agree, is to informally keep the investigation open and see if anything turns up. I'll continue to do it pro bono. Unless I'm successful, Charles may spend the rest of his life in prison."

On his way back to Toronto, Ed phoned Pamela Huntsman. She didn't answer, so he left a long message hoping that he would be able to visit with her the next day before he and Annie headed back to Lighthouse Cove.

When Ed walked into the hotel room, Annie, swathed chin to ankle in a thick white terry cloth robe, greeted him with a glass of wine and a big kiss. "I had a fabulous day," she sighed, "and just got out of a very warm and fragrant bubble bath in that huge soaking tub in the bathroom. Did you have a bad day? You don't look very happy."

"I'd rather hear about your day first. There's some breaking news with the case, but I can tell you about it over dinner. And by the way, you look amazing. Your skin is glowing, you smell great, and you did something to your hair."

"Yes, my dear, and that is why my day was so fabulous. I started off with lunch at the café here in the hotel; then went for a walk. My first stop was to a salon where I got a manicure and pedicure and was coerced into getting a new hairdo," she fluffed at her short, choppy hairdo. "Expensive, but well worth it, as you can see. I then strolled into a couple of art galleries, saw some interesting pieces, but none that fit our décor or budget, and then browsed in some very fashionable boutiques, most of which displayed outfits more suited to anorexic 20-year-olds than someone my age."

"You didn't get a new outfit for tonight? I thought that was part of your mission."

"Well, yes I did," Annie responded, looking absolutely delighted. "I discovered Olivia's, a wonderful boutique located about three blocks from the hotel. It carried a whole array of incredible clothing that was not only interesting and different, but also designed for us older women. I walked in, told the saleswoman what I was looking for, and within minutes purchased a stunning and very age appropriate outfit to wear to dinner tonight. You will see the finished product after I get dressed."

She kissed Ed again. He smiled. "Annie, I'm so glad you had fun. I'm going to take a shower and change my clothes."

Chapter 37

Forty-five minutes later, Annie and Ed emerged
from the elevator and walked through the hotel lobby to
the street. Ed thought Annie looked sensational in a
black velvet long-sleeved tunic with black satin cuffs
and neckline and black silk pants. Her accessories
included jet pear-shaped earrings rimmed with
sparkling crystals and a wide jet cuff. High-heeled
black leather boots completed the look. She'd donned
an ankle-length black cashmere coat with a faux mink
shawl collar for the short walk to the restaurant.

Under a double-breasted camel-hair overcoat, Ed
wore a dark suit, oxford blue shirt and yellow and blue
patterned tie. Annie told him he looked like a very
distinguished version of an aging James Bond.

Snow had started to fall, big, wet fluffy flakes that
caught the amber glow of the street lights and then
melted into small puddles on the sidewalk and street.
The restaurant, located on the first floor of a four-story
brownstone that nestled cozily between two imposing
multi-storied red brick and limestone skyscrapers,
glowed inside with white tablecloths, crystal
chandeliers and low lighting provided by pewter and
glass wall sconces. On each table, a small, square
crystal vase held a shimmering, ivory-colored votive
candle.

The maître'd welcomed the pair, led them to their
table, and pulled out chairs to seat them. Within
seconds their server greeted them and after reciting the
evening's specials took their drink orders.

Annie requested a glass of white burgundy, and Ed, a Talisker, his favorite single malt scotch. While waiting for the escargot in puff pastry they'd ordered as an appetizer, Annie said, "Okay, now spill. What happened today?"

Ed quickly summarized his interview with Jennifer Ashwani and reported that the university possessed the authentic map and a manuscript that had been discovered at an architectural dig. He said she gave him a copy although he'd been told little about its contents.

"That's so exciting, Ed! I'd like to read it when you're finished. I may be able to weave some of the information into our own history and purchase some copies of the manuscript to sell in the gift store."

Ed then told her about his conversation with Angelica Hawthorn and Charles' confession.

"Carrie and I think he could be lying and covering for someone, but unless we can prove it and find out who really killed her, Charles is likely to spend the rest of his life in jail. I'll give you all the salient details tomorrow on our drive home, but if you're okay with it, I'd really like to keep tonight for ourselves."

"I'm fine with that, but poor Charles." Annie sighed. "It's never made sense to me that he would murder Emily, and I'm glad you and Carrie are at least now willing to consider that someone else may have done it. I think he's covering for someone, too. But who?"

"That's the big question, isn't it? It may take some time, but I promise you I'll continue the investigation until we find out one way or the other."

The couple sat in silence while they ate the escargot, which was followed by an amuse bouche lemon and thyme sorbet. They had ordered a bottle of Cotes du Rhone and sipped it slowly, while Ed savored his meal of braised lamb with winter vegetables, risotto and green salad and Annie waxed poetic over the chicken

Marengo, creamy polenta and a salad of greens, roasted beets, candied pecans and sections of fresh mandarin orange. A steaming double espresso for Ed and a decaf cappuccino for Annie rounded out their dinner, both too full to sample the tantalizing array of desserts and cheeses presented for their purview on a silver platter.

Once back at the hotel, Ed changed into a long-sleeved cotton tee shirt and flannel sleeping pants, and with the manuscript in hand was just getting ready to sit in one of a pair of easy chairs facing the television when Annie emerged from the bathroom wearing a floor-length silver-colored satin nightgown with a low-cut bodice and spaghetti straps.

"Wow!" Ed whistled as she pirouetted before him and then gave him a coquettish wink of the eye. He laughed. "I think I'll read the manuscript some other time," he said, guiding her to the bed. "After all these years," he said throatily, "you still knock my socks off."

Many minutes later Annie sighed and stretched. "Wow, is right," she gave a husky laugh. "And you, after all these years, are still the sexiest man I know."

"Much sexier than James Bond," she murmured. Ed grinned, stroked her hair and pulled her close. Nestling like spoons, they both fell into a deep, untroubled sleep.

Chapter 38

The next morning, Ed and Annie decided to take a faster route home by crossing over the Rainbow Bridge near Buffalo. They had just passed through customs when Ed's cell phone rang. He switched to Blue Tooth and answered it. "This is Ed."

"Mr. DeCleryk, this is Pam Huntsman. I'm so sorry I didn't return your call yesterday. I taught three classes, had a faculty meeting and then rushed home to feed my two children while my husband picked up the babysitter so he and I could attend the parent-teacher conferences at their school. By the time we got home it was after nine, and I didn't want to disrupt your evening. Are you still in Toronto?"

"No. We're on our way back to Lighthouse Cove. Did you listen to my voice message?"

"Yes, and I'm happy to help you any way I can. What's the best way to do this?"

"Can I call you later this afternoon?"

"That's not going to work. I have classes and meetings all day, plus a faculty reception tonight. How about between 9:30 and 10:30 tomorrow morning? You can call me on this line, which is the one Angelica gave you. I'm quite curious about this whole situation and will do anything I can to help, especially if the results mean exonerating Charles. He mentored me, and I have to say he's the last person I'd suspect as a murderer."

"None of us wants him to be guilty, Pamela, and please, call me Ed. Any info you can give will be much appreciated."

In the meantime, Carrie, acting on a hunch, had decided to call the crime lab to double check if they might have missed finding paint flecks, possibly from the radiator, in Emily's scalp. The tech reiterated that there was nothing in the report indicating anything other than the cast iron splinters. But he had a thought.

"Maybe you want to go over to the museum and check that radiator again," he suggested. "Maybe it was never painted, or the paint could have been chipped off where your victim fell against it."

"Good idea. Ben gave me the code to the keypad before he left, so I'll go over right now and check things out. I'm sure Annie won't mind."

Several minutes later, Carrie called the tech back. "The radiator is painted, so it's not what Emily fell against that knocked her out. The light in that office isn't very bright, and the office is also very small so maybe Charles thought she hit her head on it when she fell but she didn't, and when she fell in the basement she fell back against the scuttle instead of being hit from behind, as we surmised."

She sighed. "The discrepancies between Charles' story and our assumptions notwithstanding, it looks like Charles' confession will hold up despite our suspicion that he's covering for the real killer. I'll call Ed and let him know."

Before she called Ed, Carrie questioned Charles once more, trying to get him to talk about the coal scuttle, but even leading questions didn't yield the information she was hoping for. Charles insisted that he had pushed Emily and that he believed she had hit her head on the radiator.

Ed and Annie had stopped for lunch in Rochester when Carrie's call came in. After hanging up, he told Annie about their conversation, the details of Charles' confession and that he would be arraigned on a charge of second degree murder. She looked puzzled.

"There's more than one thing about all of this that just doesn't make sense, Ed. Now for sure I know he's lying."

"Why is that?"

She told him, and he responded, "I don't get it."

"Well, neither do I. Something is very off here."

"Even if he's not guilty of killing Emily, Annie, he's constructed a believable confession. I wish the outcome had been different, but what you just told me isn't enough to prove his innocence unless I can find out who really killed Emily."

Annie, pensive, sat in silence on the ride home to Lighthouse Cove from Rochester. Later, she declined Ed's offer of a glass of wine and asked him if he minded fending for himself for dinner. For most of the evening she sat in the living room staring at the fire.

Ed knew how fond Annie was of Charles and that she was upset and terribly disappointed. When ready, she'd talk to him, but for now she needed to be left alone so she could work out her feelings. Ed picked up the manuscript and carried it into his study where he put on his reading glasses, settled into the leather recliner and began to read.

Chapter 39

From Thomas Battleforth's Manuscript:

I was born and raised on an estate northwest of London where my parents served as gamekeeper and governess for Lord and Lady Hollingsworth. A generous man, the lord allowed me at a very young age to join the children, Jane and Alden, in their studies. I learned to read, write and do math sums, and my early years were happy and peaceful. My life changed shortly after my ninth birthday.

On a late afternoon in November while walking through the forest, my father, Peter, was attacked by a wild boar that gored him through his belly. No amount of care could save him, and in just a few days he left our known world and went to heaven to be with our Savior. My mother, Lydia, and I grieved sorely for him, but the lord and lady assured us that our place with the family was secure, and our life continued much as it had before, but without the strong and caring presence of our loving husband and father.

Several years passed in this manner when one day, Lord Hollingsworth announced that a cousin from Cornwall, Viscount Evensong, would be joining the family for a fortnight. The staff worked hard to air out the guest and servants' quarters to make them ready as he would be bringing with him his household staff and his groomsman.

He appeared on a sunny April morning. His carriage safely sheltered, horses liveried and trunk of belongings taken to his quarters to be unpacked, he walked through the main hall to greet the household staff who had assembled to welcome him to the estate. That he was a handsome man could not be missed. He stood tall and slender, dressed in trim pants, a billowing waistcoat and short jacket, his dark hair pulled back and held against his neck by a ribbon. We were told later by some of the kitchen staff that he had not yet wed. We guessed his age at about 30.

He stopped in front of my mother and smiled, his pale gray eyes shining and the dimple in his chin widening. "Now aren't you a lovely thing," he said, taking her hand, his eyes sweeping the length of her body. "What may I call you?"

My mother, indeed very comely with shining blond hair, large, dark-lashed hazel eyes and a trim figure replied, "I'm the governess, sir, and my name is Lydia Battleforth. This is my son, Thomas." She put her arm around me and nudged me toward him. I bowed as I took his proffered hand. "Why, aren't you a strapping young man," he exclaimed. "How many years are you?"

"Almost thirteen, sir," I replied.

"And where is your father, Thomas? Will you soon be joining him in his service?"

"My father was the gamekeeper here, sir. He died. He was gored by a boar."

"Then soon it will be time for you to leave your mother and find service elsewhere," he remarked.

For some reason, a chill settled upon me, but I replied, "I suppose so, my lord."

He smiled again at my mother before moving down the line. A deeper sense of foreboding than I'd ever felt went through me.

When my parents met and fell in love, Lord Hollingsworth gave his permission for them to marry and allowed my mother to live with my father in the gamekeeper's cottage, a humble dwelling with a sitting room, cooking hearth and two private rooms for sleeping. It was located a short distance from the children's quarters in the west wing of the manor house.

After my father's death, my mother and I were relocated to new quarters inside the house with a smaller sitting room and two curtained sleeping alcoves—my mother's the larger of the two. Two large windows at one end looked down upon the rose garden, a door with no lock gave privacy from the hallway and to the back stairs that led to the lower floors and the kitchen, where we now took our meals with the other help.

One evening after we retired, I heard floor boards creaking in the hall, and then the door opened. Startled, I looked out from my bed and saw a tall, thin figure moving stealthily toward me and then felt a hand on my mouth.

"If you say as much as a word about this, I'll make sure you never spend a day longer at this estate. You'll end up in gaol, convicted of thievery. Now close your eyes tightly and pretend that nothing is amiss." The voice I knew was that of our guest, the Viscount Evensong.

My mother had been sleeping deeply. I could hear her regular breathing, but then she gasped, and I heard her struggle against the covers. The viscount grunted and thrashed for a few minutes and then went still. I heard him tell my mother that if she valued her life and mine that she would never say a word about what had occurred. Then he took his leave. My mother, wraithlike, continued to look after the lord and lady's children during the day, the viscount's unwanted visits continuing each night.

Several days after the viscount's arrival, Lady Hollingsworth asked my mother to join her after breakfast in her morning room. "My dear," said the lady, expressing concern, "you have not been looking well. Are you perhaps ill?"

"No, my lady, just weary. I will be fine."

"Well then, make sure you take to your sleeping quarters earlier for the next couple of nights," she advised, gliding away.

At the end of a fortnight, the viscount took his leave, but my mother never recovered from his nightly attacks. Ashamed, she would not look directly at me, and she walked about hunched over like an old woman, pale and wan. Then the sickness began. Not able to eat, she grew thin, and when questioned by the other staff or the lord and lady, she made excuses which I knew to be fabrications, but which they chose at first to believe. I had seen rutting animals and heard the noises they made while mating, and I correctly guessed what had occurred between my mother and Viscount Evensong and that she was with child.

After a few months the sickness stopped, and she began to gain weight, most of it in her belly. I feared for her, and one day my fear was realized when Lady Hollingsworth called my dear mother into her withdrawing room. I stood outside the door and eavesdropped.

"You have been out of sorts for months now, Lydia," she said.

"Yes, my lady."

"I notice that your belly has begun to swell. Are you, perhaps with child?"

Bowing her head, my mother responded, "Yes, my lady."

"And who is the father, Lydia?"

"I cannot tell you," my mother said weakly.

"Will this person who has made you with child do what's honorable and wed you?"

"We shall never marry, my lady. That is quite impossible."

"Shame, shame, Lydia. I had thought you of a higher personage than you in fact seem to be. Have you consorted with a servant, a craftsman, perhaps a merchant in the town?"

"I cannot say, my lady."

"You don't know who fathered your babe, Lydia? That is appalling. When your husband was alive I thought you were a faithful and loving wife and had no idea of your baser nature. We do not abide promiscuity here, Lydia, and I cannot have my children affected by your lack of morality. You shall be dismissed immediately without character."

My mother, dismayed beyond reason, turned ashen as she shed tears as abundantly as a river. "Please, my lady. I have not been promiscuous as you believe. I was taken against my will. What shall I do?"

"I am sorry to hear that, but unless you tell me who violated you, so we can force him to marry you for the sake of the unborn child and our family's reputation, I have no choice but to release you from service. After that, what you do is of no consequence to me. Because you have heretofore served us well, I will wait to set you out until you have made other arrangements. You have a fortnight."

"I simply cannot tell you who the father is, and marriage would not be possible," my mother cried, knowing full well that if she disclosed the name of her violator she would not be believed.

Lady Hollingsworth merely shook her head and left the withdrawing room, my mother standing by her chair, sobbing. By courier, my mother sent notice to her sister, who lived in Wales with her husband, that she had been dismissed but chose not to explain the circumstances of her dismissal in the letter. Kind-hearted, and without questioning the reason, my aunt and uncle opened their home to us, and on a rainy autumn day we set off to begin a new life.

My mother and aunt were close, my uncle a warm and decent man, and they made room for us in their home and in their hearts. Both were outraged when they heard the story of my mother's violation, but there was no possible way to take revenge. The ruling classes viewed even the most refined and educated among us as chattel. To give us respectability, the story they told the villagers was that my father had recently died leaving us destitute, my mother pregnant with their second child. While I missed sorely my old life, I felt secure once again, and the months passed quickly before my mother's lying in.

Now, at the age of thirteen, I would need to earn my keep and take care of my mother and the new babe. Without a letter vouching for her character, she would be unable to support us unless she went to a workhouse or took to the streets, and I knew my aunt and uncle never would abide that.

I asked my uncle for his counsel on how I might earn a livelihood. He worked as a blacksmith, but I had no aptitude for that, and we talked about my taking a position at a local estate, perhaps as a gamekeeper, like my father had done. But without a letter of character that avenue also was closed to me.

I liked the sea. My mother and I had accompanied the lord, lady and their children to their estate in Brighton on a short holiday the summer after my father died, and I never forgot it, vowing to return when I grew older. After making some inquiries, my uncle discovered that the captain of a ship leaving for the former colonies in America, was looking to hire a cabin boy. A friend of my uncle, he was willing to take me into service based on my uncle's word that I was of strong character. While I didn't want to leave my mother, I knew that my childhood must end and agreed to meet with the captain, planning to leave for London within several days.

One night I awoke out of a sound sleep to hear my mother screaming. I ran into her room and found my aunt holding her hand and wiping her fevered brow. "It seems," she said, "as though the babe is coming, too soon, before its time. Now leave us, Thomas. I will come for you after the babe is delivered."

The screaming continued and after one last shriek, the cottage became very silent. I ran into my mother's room and saw blood everywhere. A tiny, deformed girl-child lay on my dear, sweet-tempered dead mother's belly; my aunt weeping upon her still breast.

*****

Engrossed in the story, Ed didn't hear Annie come into the room. "I'm sorry," she said. "I thought more about Charles and his confession, and I just can't believe he killed Emily."

Ed closed the book and put it on the table beside him. He stood up and pulled Annie close to him, and she snuggled her small frame against him.

He sighed. "You and Carrie have always believed in Charles' innocence, and you may be correct. I promise to continue to work the case to see if anything surfaces that could exonerate Charles, but don't get your hopes up. If it gets to trial, the prosecutor will convincingly argue that Charles could have been confused or gotten a bit mixed up about some of the details when he confessed, but his story could still be viewed as credible. This is tough for all of us, and I know it is especially for you. Please don't hold your feelings in. I know you needed be alone tonight, but remember, I'm always here for you."

"Thank you." Annie put her head against his chest and sighed. "If this ever does go to trial, I won't go, you know. I couldn't bear to be there." He nodded. She noticed the manuscript on the table.

"So, are you enjoying it? Is it interesting?"

"Compelling, actually. I'm just getting into the heart of the story but have no idea how at this point the map will figure into it. But it's enough reading for now. I'll continue tomorrow."

Chapter 40

Ed, Carrie, and Suzanne's friend, Garrett, who had agreed to represent Charles, were present the next morning at his arraignment. He was charged, as they had expected, with second-degree murder, but Garrett convinced the DA to drop pending burglary charges since Charles had technically entered the museum lawfully and hadn't stolen anything. He also convinced Charles to change his plea to not guilty, confident he could successfully argue for an acquittal.

Charles voluntarily surrendered his passport, and the judge set bail at $50,000. Against Garrett's advice, he declined to post it and was remanded, according to his wishes, to the county jail.

Carrie and Ed shook their heads in disbelief.

*****

At the appointed time, Ed called Pam Huntsman. "Are you able to talk?"

"Yes, my kids are in school, and I'm free, no classes today. What can I do for you?"

Ed went into more detail about why he was calling and told Pam that Charles had been charged with second-degree murder.

"That's so sad," Pam responded. "I can't believe he's guilty."

"Is there anything you can you tell me that might help us exonerate him?"

"I don't know," she responded. "I can tell you about our trip to Lighthouse Cove, although there's probably nothing I know that you don't." She gave Ed the same version as Angelica's of the events from the map discovery to the trip to Lighthouse Cove.

She continued, "As you may know, at first Charles challenged the opinion of some of the others on the team but then relented because he trusted their professional expertise. I argued we should ask the historical society for permission to do a mini-excavation anyway, just in case there was something buried there, but they were adamant it would be a waste of time. We had a student with us, Michael Warren, but he had no skin in the game. He came with us because he was writing a feature story about Charles for the school newspaper."

"Angelica Hawthorn told me Samantha Chu moved to British Columbia and that she thought Barry Eaton still worked for the Toronto Planning Commission. Do you know if that's true?" asked Ed.

"Yes. I can get you their contact info, but I'm positive neither he nor Sam would be involved in this. Sam wouldn't travel all the way from BC to conduct a surreptitious excavation in the middle of the night, and Barry seemed annoyed about having to make the trip in the first place. They both thought the trip was a waste of time."

"I have to ask this, it's just a formality, but where were you on the night of the murder?"

"No problem. I have nothing to hide. I was at a department committee meeting until about 10:30 and then went home, watched the late news with my husband, and went to bed. I was back here the next morning at about 7:30 because I had an 8 a.m. class. You can check with my department head and some of my students."

"Not necessary, but thank you. Do you know where Michael Warren is?"

"I think he may be living in South Korea. He majored in English. I ran into him just before he graduated, and he told me he was going to spend a few years teaching English as a second language at a private school in the Gangnam district in Seoul."

"Were you the one who arranged for his interview with Charles?"

"I was. I met Michael at a party that was hosted by a friend who's an English professor. Michael knew Charles by reputation, and when he learned that I was Charles' teaching assistant asked me if I thought he might be willing to be interviewed for a feature in the paper. I asked Charles, who was agreeable and suggested it might be a good experience for me to sit in, and I arranged for Michael to meet with him. Charles mentioned the trip to Lighthouse Cove, Michael asked if he could tag along, make it part of the story, and Charles consented."

"Anything unusual happen during the interview?"

"No. It was very cordial. They made small talk at first. I think Charles orchestrated it to put Michael at ease because he appeared to be a bit nervous. Michael noticed some photos on Charles' credenza, and seemed taken by one with a much younger Charles and two friends standing at a dock, smiling and holding up three huge steelhead trout."

"I know that photo," Ed responded. "He has it displayed on the mantel in his living room."

Pamela continued, "Michael asked him where the photo was taken, and Charles told him that when he was in his 50s he had spent a summer in Ithaca doing research at Cornell, and that one weekend he and a couple of colleagues had taken a trip to the Thousand Islands, which is where they caught the fish.

"Michael remarked that he'd been raised in Ithaca, and they agreed it was a small world, although Charles didn't recognize the family name. Charles asked Michael if he liked to fish, and he said he did and that he used to fish with his father but that his parents had moved to Chicago and with him now going to school in Toronto, they weren't able to do that as often as they used to. Charles said maybe the two of them could go fishing sometime, Michael said he'd like that, and then he started the interview."

"Would you mind calling the alumni office and see if you can get Michael's contact information? I'd like to talk with him to see what, if anything, he remembers about the trip here and whether he and Charles actually went on the fishing trip."

"I can try, but unless he sends updates, that information may not be correct."

"That's fine. If I'm able to talk with him that would be great, but he's really peripheral to my investigation."

"Let me see what I can do."

Ed thanked Pamela, hung up and began calling the others who were with Charles on the exploratory trip to the states. As he expected, they all had airtight alibis and none of them had had any communication with Charles in the past or present that would lead them to believe he could have gone into the museum to conduct his own excavation.

Ed's phone rang several hours later. It was Pamela. "Last thing the alumni office knew, Michael was still in South Korea, but they haven't had any communication from him for more than a year. The only contact info he gave was an email address, but that may not be current."

"Thanks. I'll email him and tell him what's going on and ask if he'd be willing to give me a phone number and let me call him. I expect he won't be able to tell me anything I don't know already, but I'd still like to speak with him, if possible."

"Good luck, Ed. I really hope you can find a way to get the charges dropped for Charles."

Ed emailed Michael Warren with details about who he was and why he wanted to speak with him. If he responded, fine; if not, he wasn't going to pursue it.

Chapter 41

The following morning, a snowy one, Annie visited Charles in jail. She was dismayed at how much weaker and frailer he had become, and, still puzzled about his confession, let him know she believed in his innocence.

"But Annie, I'm not innocent," he said, "and I'm quite willing to pay for my sins." Annie thought his response a bit odd. Charles looked beaten down and resigned.

"I'll be back to see you again, Charles. Do you want me to contact your family members in Canada?" Charles shook his head.

"Very well, then," Annie said. Saddened by the exchange, she left, certain that her instincts were correct and that, despite Charles' protestations to the contrary, he was not Emily's killer.

Annie joined Ed for a glass of wine before dinner that evening and told him about her visit. Over the simple meal she'd prepared of roasted lemon chicken, a green salad and a loaf of crusty bread, Ed told her about his phone conversations with the team that had accompanied Charles to Lighthouse Cove and his email to Michael Warren. He'd not yet responded, but Ed had taken into consideration the time zone difference and figured that if he did hear back from him it probably would take a day or two. Annie expressed disappointment, hoping Michael would get back to Ed quickly with new information.

"Michael may not even be in South Korea, Annie. These teaching jobs abroad sometimes are limited to a

couple of years, and for all we know he could be back
in the states or in Canada or anywhere, for that matter.
I'd probably be able to do a search for him through the
FBI and Royal Canadian Mounted Police, but I'm not
sure it's worth taking up their time.

"He also may have received the email but decided
that he just doesn't want to be involved. Admiring
Charles when he was a student is much different than
consenting to be interviewed as part of a murder
investigation."

*****

After dinner Ed sat down in his easy chair and
continued reading Thomas Battleforth's manuscript:

*"My dear mother and the poor unwanted babe were
buried two days later in a small plot behind the church
in our village. Along with the preacher and his wife,
only my aunt, uncle and I attended. A slow anger was
beginning to burn in my chest. My father's death was a
terrible accident, but my mother could have lived a long
full life if not for the Viscount Evensong, perhaps even
marrying again. Now my parents, who loved each other
without reservation, would be separated for eternity,
not even able, in death, to be joined together.*

*A few days later I summoned a carriage, bade my
aunt and uncle goodbye, and with a rucksack
containing my paltry belongings set out for the harbor
in London where I would be boarding a ship bound for
America.*

*Growing up on an estate and living for a short time
in Wales had not prepared me for London, a crowded,
dirty and noisy city. After several days traveling, we
arrived at the congested harbor at the Pool of London,
where ships filled with cargo would set sail for Spain,
France, India, and the Americas. I slowly made my way
to the Queen Charlotte, the merchant ship upon which I*

would be sailing. Throngs of filthy beggars wearing tattered rags reached out to me, pleading for food or coins and clutching at my clothing as I walked by them. I felt both frightened and sad.

Captain Willoughby, a kind but exacting man, greeted me and after giving me a tour of the ship, told me that in addition to our cargo, we would also be transporting a few select passengers across the ocean. All relatives of the royal family, they would require special care as the ship was not large enough to accommodate them and their servants, and since I had some refinements and knew how to read, write and do sums, he would be assigning me to look after them as their cabin boy. I asked about them, curious as to whom they were.

He told me, "King George wishes for a peaceful relationship with our former colonies and is sending his son, Prince Frederick, the Duke of York, and his wife, Princess Fredericka Charlotte of Prussia, to meet with Governor George Clinton of New York. Then, some days later they will board another ship, the HMS Orion, which will sail north to the St. Lawrence River and from there to Lake Ontario, heading for the Canadian settlement of York where they will meet with Governor John Graves Simcoe.

"They will be carrying letters of introduction from the king to both governors plus generous gifts of the Queen Consort's Wedgewood pottery, a ruby-encrusted snuff box for the Governor of New York, pearl earrings for his lady; a diamond, ruby and sapphire encrusted scabbard for the Governor of York and a diamond and ruby brooch for his lady. You will need to take good care, my boy, as any missteps or thievery on your part could result in your very early death by hanging."

"I understand, Captain, and am ready to serve," I demurred.

"Oh, and one more thing. They will be accompanied by the prince's cousin, to whom you will also be assigned. A real gentleman, the Viscount Evensong is."

I mustered as much strength as I could to not react to this unsettling and shocking news. At first, I thought to run far away, back to Wales and to the loving care of my aunt and uncle. But then the burning that had started in my chest grew stronger, and I vowed that before the voyage ended in Canada I would extract my revenge, although I knew not what that would be.

The next day I stood at attention as the captain greeted our royal passengers and introduced me as their cabin boy, Thomas. Fortunate for me, he gave no surname, as I feared the viscount might recognize it. As they passed, the prince and princess, haughty and entitled, barely looked at me. But the viscount stopped and stared for a moment.

"Do I know you, boy? Have we met?" he queried.

"No, my lord, I don't believe we have," I responded, looking him straight in the eye and trying to remain calm. Inwardly I trembled, both with rage and fear.

"You look somewhat familiar. From where do you hail?"

"I hail from Wales, my lord, where I lived with my aunt and uncle, who is a blacksmith. I had no aptitude for it, though, and so through his contacts, my uncle found this position for me. My mother died giving birth to my sister, and my father died shortly before her in an accident."

"Hmm, well then, for a moment I thought I recognized you."

He passed on. I spent most of the voyage caring for the royals, meeting their incessant demands. They had entrusted me to guard the treasure, which was stored in a copper box in a waxed, waterproof rucksack made from hemp with wide straps to fit over the bearer's arms. Since no one could get off or on the ship, it was safe under my keeping.

I placed it in a corner under a sheep's wool rug in the prince and princess' quarters but checked every day to make sure it was still hidden. I didn't trust the viscount who could easily have stolen the jewels and blamed me or other crew members for it, but he seemed to be perfectly content walking the decks, playing cards and indulging his quite voracious appetite for spirits and food. He was, to my amusement and satisfaction, becoming quite stout.

The voyage passed without crisis. We finally, after many weeks, reached our destination. After anchoring in the vast New York harbor, our royal passengers were greeted by emissaries of Governor Clinton and escorted, with the locked copper box still inside the rucksack now borne by the Governor's servants, to his mansion where they visited for several days.

Pleased with my attention to them, the captain gave me some coins and a few days leave, and I passed my time exploring the city with sailors and cabin boys from ours and other ships who helped me gain an understanding of, among other worldly delights, the pleasures of womanly flesh, and thus I gained my manhood.

Dismissed of my duties on the Queen Charlotte, which by now had begun its return journey back to England, I now signed on to the HMS Orion as the royals' cabin boy, something heretofore agreed upon by all concerned. A few days later, the ship set sail for Canada with the prince, princess, viscount and copper box containing gifts for the Governor of York and his lady.

*****

Ed put the journal down, stood up, stretched, and walked into the kitchen to make himself a cup of tea. So

far, the manuscript was an interesting read, but there
were no clues about how it was related to the map or
some of Charles Merrill's comments. Annie walked
into the kitchen and asked him if he wanted to watch
TV with her. PBS was airing a live performance of the
classic musical, *Les Miserables*, with some of the
original cast, she told him.

He shook his head. "Thanks, but I'm going to pass."
He held up the manuscript. "It's been a pretty
interesting story so far, and I'd like to finish it tonight if
possible. If there are any clues in it that can help us get
Charles out of jail, the sooner the better. Enjoy the
performance."

Ed settled into the chair again and continued
reading:

*"The trip to the North Atlantic and through the St.
Lawrence River was pleasant. The wind held steady, we
made good time, and the days were sunny and bright.
But by the time we reached Lake Ontario, choppy and
fickle and deep, the wind had picked up, creating high
waves that rocked our ship like a babe's cradle out of
control.*

*Most of the crew, and the royal passengers, fell ill.
For some reason, my sea legs held steady, so along
with emptying chamber pots, I now had the added
responsibility of cleaning up after the sick. Grateful
crew praised and thanked me but our royal passengers,
ever entitled and with the assumption that I would look
after them under any circumstances, paid me no notice.
I could barely contain my ever-growing rage.*

*During the trip from England I had found no
opportunity for revenge, nor could I come up with a
plan. But now, with the wind growing stronger, a sliver
of an idea came into my head. I prayed for a storm and
one evening was granted my wish.*

At just after dusk, the sky, already darkened, grew even darker, and a fierce storm, with howling winds, cannon-like thunder, sharp crackling bolts of lighting and waves so high that they crashed over the bow and stern of the ship, moved in, tossing the boat in the water as though it were a twig in a river with rapids.

Alarmed for the safety of his passengers, the captain ushered the royals into his quarters, along with as many crew as could fit into the space. The prince instructed me to get the treasure and bring it to him. It was then that I knew that I would never return to England.

Relations between the French and English had long been strained and when the French sympathized with and fought alongside the colonists during the American War of Revolution, they became increasingly more so. I believed the French might be willing to pay a very pretty penny for jewels belonging to King George, in part as reparations for the aid they had given the colonists during the war. I could live my life in a remote area of Canada, a free and wealthy man, never having to submit again to the whims of unscrupulous and evil royals.

A lull in the storm brought stillness and quiet, but I knew it was the calm that precedes more turbulence. It was then that I made my decision. I crept into the royal couple's chambers, placed the straps of the rucksack containing the box with the treasures through my arms, but instead of returning with it to the captain's quarters, I took a rope and tied it around the sack and to my waist and quickly threw a life barge over the side of ship and into the churning water.

I jumped into the barge and started paddling away, waves washing over me, almost drowning me in the process. Through God's grace the barge held tight, but the storm had started again, with more fierce thunder and lighting, and as I looked back I saw a massive bolt hit the ship.

Flames shot up towards the darkened sky, and I heard a creaking, cracking noise such as I had never heard before and watched as the ship began to burn and then dismantle and break apart, taking all the passengers with it into the graveyard of the sea. They would never know of my deception.

Chapter 42

Ed, by now thoroughly engrossed with the story, wanted to finish it; but he took a quick break to stretch, put his mug in the dishwasher and check on Annie, who was absorbed with the TV show and didn't hear him walk into the family room. Not wanting to interrupt her, he went back into his study, picked up the manuscript and continued to read:

"I awoke on a rocky beach, drenched, shivering but alive. Astoundingly, the rucksack was still secured against me. Dawn was beginning to break, and in the distance, I saw the stirring of morning activity, cabins with smoke curling into the sky from chimneys, cows grazing in fields. I had no idea where I was, and not trusting that the settlers would be friendly, I removed the copper box from the rucksack, dragged myself up the short bluff where at the top stood a wooden lighthouse, and using a flattened rock like a spade dug a deep hole in a bed of wildflowers that grew along one side of the edifice, buried the box, filled the hole with dirt, and covered it with stones and grass. Then I collapsed.

Sometime later, I awoke on a narrow bed in a square, clean room with whitewashed walls and a window overlooking the bay, and was told by a small, round woman with kind eyes and a tall, slight man with a pleasant face that a group of villagers, fishing for their daily meal, had found me on the bluff five days before, my rucksack emptied of my possessions.

Fever burning up my body and delirious, I had no memory that they had carried me into the small settlement and brought me to the home of my hosts, Levi DeCleryk, the village preacher, and his wife, Sara, who nursed me with poultices and sips of broth until the fever broke. They said in my ramblings I cried out the names Lydia and Peter and that I talked about living in Canada.

I told them that Lydia and Peter were my parents; that they were English born but no longer lived there, and these kind people assumed they had immigrated to Canada. I didn't disabuse them of their assumption.

The settlement, called Lighthouse Cove, was located on the southern shores of Lake Ontario in New York. The residents, all patriots during the Revolution, bore me no ill will, for although some Canadians fought against them in the war, they mainly blamed England and its rulers for resisting their demand for independence.

Upon questioning I told them about the shipwreck but fabricated the story, saying that I had been a cabin boy on the ship that had left Canada en route to the St. Lawrence River to meet up with a schooner that would take the prince, princess and viscount back to England after a visit with the Governor of York. They had no cause to misbelieve me and besides, the HMS Orion as it turned out, had been a war ship that had fired upon these very people during the revolution. Few expressed sadness at its demise or that of its royal passengers, although they prayed for the innocent lives that had been lost with them, as I did for the ship's kind and amiable captain.

One week followed another. I grew stronger and began to help with family chores that included looking after the cattle and working in the fruit orchards and vineyards. I began to feel well and content again and started to think that perhaps I had erred in my plan to seek freedom in Canada and determined I would remain in this peaceful village with these kind and caring villagers. Once again, my life took a turn in a different direction.

One day a ship sailed into the harbor, and while I watched it anchor, Sara, eyes bright with joy, told me that arrangements had been made for me to make passage on it. On the morrow, it would continue its journey to York, where, she told me, I could be reunited with my parents who must be brokenhearted thinking I had drowned when the ship went down in the storm. I had no alternative but to obey them unless they discover that my story had been a lie, and humbly thanking them for their hospitality, I set off for a new adventure.

As part of the recovery from my illness, I had been encouraged to spend parts of my days out of doors, enjoying the fresh sea air. I always was accompanied by one villager or another who kept a close eye on me, expressing concern for my well-being and safety. Sometimes our walks took us past the spot where I had buried the treasure, but I never had the opportunity to return alone.

I had observed the shoreline and the shape of the village, and once on board the ship, I asked for a quill, some ink and paper and began to draw a map of the area, marking the spot where the treasure was buried. My plan was to go back some day and find a way to dig it up, but that never was to be.

The voyage to York was a pleasant one, and a cabin boy and I struck up a friendship. I told him about the shipwreck, and that I had been orphaned, and he told me he and his family had emigrated from England and lived in a remote settlement north of York, consisting mainly of traders and trappers. His name was Simon

Merrill, and he offered that I dwell for a time with him, his parents and sister, Rebecca, until I was at last able to sustain myself.

The small community welcomed me, and I quickly settled into life there, learning first the trade of a hostler. After many years, an epidemic of flux and pox and pestilence invaded this settlement like flies around a carcass, and I discovered an aptitude for healing.

Our friends and neighbors, the Cayuga Indians, taught me to use all manner of things: herbs as draughts to cure fever and flux, the bark of the willow tree to ease pain, grains and mud as poultices, plant leaves as emetics. Soon I became a respected healer, earning my keep through the generosity of the settlers who kept me well fed, sheltered and prosperous. My life settled into a calm and happy routine.

Rebecca, Simon's lovely sister, with flaxen hair and hazel eyes that reminded me of my mother, learned that she, too, had the healing gifts and worked alongside me. Soon we realized that the bond between us was far greater than that of two healers. We wed and began our family—three sons and two daughters—who unlike many of the children in the settlement, grew to their maturity. Before I knew it, the years passed and all the thoughts of revenge and the stolen treasure with them. My life was finally happy.

Now, in my 75th year, I have told this story. I'm an old man and have no thoughts of when our Lord will take me, but I live each day in contentment, my beloved wife at my side, our many children and grandchildren nearby. None of them knows about the map, which I have hidden securely in a metal box beneath our stone hearth, but every so often with no others at hand, I pull it out and gaze at it, not sorry I never had a chance to go back for the treasure but with guilt and regret that I had stolen it. I hope, should it ever be found, that it will

be returned to its rightful owner, the monarchy of England, for whom I no longer bear ill will.
Thomas Battleforth.
Toronto, Canada 1847

*****

Ed, incredulous, closed the book and put it on a bookshelf in his study. Sniffling and wiping her teary eyes as her TV program ended, Annie turned to him as he walked into the family room. "Well?" she asked.

"This is unbelievable. I understand why Charles wanted so desperately to find the treasure and why it would have been difficult for him to concede that it might not be buried in Lighthouse Cove. I also learned that my ancestors were responsible for getting Thomas Battleforth, the author of this manuscript who became Charles' relative by marriage, to Canada. Sadly, learning what happened doesn't get me any closer to finding clues to prove he's innocent. Despite the gaps in his story, his confession may hold up."

He gave Annie a synopsis but said to her, "You'll really want to read this."

Shortly after, they went to bed.

Chapter 43

The next morning, Ed called Angelica Hawthorn. "Gee, thanks for holding out on me," he said wryly, after identifying himself.

She laughed. "I didn't want to spoil the fun of your reading the manuscript by giving you *all* the details, especially after I realized that Levi and Sara DeCleryk were most likely your ancestors."

"That was certainly a surprise." He paused. "I need to tell you something. Charles confessed yesterday to killing Emily Bradford and has been charged with second-degree murder."

Angelica gasped. "I can't believe it. Charles is not a murderer."

"Well, despite all-around skepticism from virtually everyone who knows him, the details he gave of how she was killed seem credible."

"I'm so sorry to hear that. What could possibly have been his motive?"

"It apparently wasn't premeditated. It seems like he reconsidered and determined that the treasure might, in fact, be in the museum. He was there early one morning to do some exploratory digging when our victim surprised him, and then the whole situation went haywire and resulted in an accident that ultimately resulted in her death.

"Unfortunately for some very misguided reasons, he decided to not report it and then disposed of the body to cover up what happened. His confession does have some gaps in it, so we're also wondering if he's covering for someone."

"As terrible as that would be, I hope it's true. If you could find out who it is, Charles might not have to serve any major time in prison. If no one else surfaces, is there any possibility that the defense attorney could claim the medication he's on for the Parkinson's disease might have caused some sort of psychotic break? I simply won't believe that Charles, if in his right mind, would intentionally cause someone's death."

"I expect his defense attorney will explore that option and others, but in the meantime, unless someone else comes forth to confess, the charge will stand."

Ed heard Angelica sigh deeply. She asked, "Can you please keep me posted about the legal proceedings? I'll want to get in touch with Charles to offer some support."

"Of course. Quick question, just out of curiosity. I can understand how Charles might have surmised that he was related to Rebecca and Simon Merrill, but why would he have been so invested in trying to find the stolen goods when Battleforth wasn't his blood relative? His theft wouldn't have reflected badly on the Merrill family. Battleforth's wife, Rebecca, had no idea what he had done."

"Well, that's where this gets interesting, Ed. After Charles read the manuscript, he was curious about whether he might be related to Rebecca and Simon, so he took a subscription to Ancestry.com. He traced his Merrill roots back to England and then in the 1700s to York, now Toronto, and determined that he was in fact related to that branch of the Merrill clan. What he didn't expect, but discovered at the same time, was that he was also related to the Battleforths.

"If you remember, he was willing to abide by the decision of the other experts when they initially determined that the treasure couldn't be buried underneath the museum. He may have changed his mind after he learned about his familial connection to Rebecca's husband."

"So, regardless of whether Charles killed Emily or is covering for someone who did, this whole chain of events began because he was determined to try and right a wrong done by his ancestor before he died."

"I expect that's correct," Angelica responded. "How tragic. Charles has always been an enigma, and unless someone else surfaces as the killer, you may never know the real story about what happened that morning."

Chapter 44

After Ed and Angelica completed their call, Ed
called Carrie and asked her to meet him at the Bistro for
coffee. It was a gray day with thick clouds that
obscured the sun and dulled the white snow covering
the ground. They arrived simultaneously and picked a
small table against a window overlooking the lake.
After ordering coffee and some pastries, Ed described
the contents of the manuscript, related how his
ancestors had helped Battleforth get from Lighthouse
Cove to Canada, and indicated that Charles was a
descendant of both the Merrills and the Battleforths.

"I promised Annie I'd continue to investigate to see
if anyone else might have been involved in Emily's
murder, but after reading the manuscript, it's also very
possible Charles is telling the truth," Ed remarked.

"Remember that at first, when the geologist and
surveyor told him that the treasure couldn't possibly be
buried somewhere inside the museum, he supported
their decision even though he was disappointed. But
then, after he discovered his relationship to both
families probably reconsidered and decided to revisit
the issue, perhaps thinking that maybe an
archaeological excavation would be appropriate after
all."

He continued, "If we believe his confession, then we
can surmise he must have been getting ready go
downstairs to look at the site where he thought the
treasure might be when he heard Emily come into the
building and, as he told us, thinking it was an intruder,

fled to the basement. He'd have probably eventually told her what he was doing, but while he was hiding and she came down to see what the noise was and tripped and fell, his anxiety level must have been off the charts. I believe him when he says her death was an accident. If he had known she was still alive, he never would have thrown her over the bluff, and he might even be regarded as a hero for saving her. How tragic that he didn't call 911 after she fell."

"It's a horrible story, Ed, and it could all have been averted if Charles had only spoken with the board of directors about his hunch and requested they explore the possibility of doing some sort of dig. Annie would know better than I, but I bet there's grant money out there for something like that. Or volunteers with archaeological expertise."

"Angelica told me the team had decided not to contact anyone in England unless there was a reason to believe the treasure really was buried within the museum, and after their trip here they were convinced it wasn't. But the jewels must be worth a fortune, plus think about their historical value. If there's a remote possibility they're there, some foundation in England might be willing to help fund an excavation. I'll tell Annie what's happened and see if she wants to take this to her board. It would be tragic if the treasure was never found because of a group of stubborn archaeologists."

"There's still something that puzzles me, Ed. We still don't know why the facsimile map was found between the two boxes in the basement. That just doesn't jive with Charles' story."

"And that's something we may never know, Carrie."

Chapter 45

By the time Ed returned home, Annie had finished reading the manuscript. "I couldn't put it down," she said. "And to think your family figured into the story and that Rebecca Merrill could be one of Charles' ancestors really boggles my mind."

Ed reprised his conversation with Angelica Hawthorn and how Charles' search on Ancestry.com proved he was related to both the Merrills and the Battleforths.

"Then I really don't get what's going on with him, Ed. After he discovered who his ancestors were why didn't he talk with me? I certainly would have supported an excavation, and I expect our board would have, too."

"Angelica Hawthorn said Charles is an enigma. Maybe that's the best answer we're going to get. Carrie and I spoke a little while ago, and we were both wondering if perhaps conducting an excavation on the site might still be possible if you could get some archaeologists to volunteer their time or grant money could be secured to do it."

"The University of Toronto, Cornell, or a foundation in England or here in upstate New York might be interested in helping us," Annie replied. "Of course, the risk, and probability, is that we'd come up empty-handed and our efforts would be wasted. But it's still worth pursuing. I need to run this by the board, and if they agree, I'll do some checking. It could take time, though, so I wouldn't expect any quick answers." Annie walked over to her computer and starting a file, began to make some notes.

"I want to write down as much as I can, so I don't forget anything. One way to start would be for me to contact Donna. She might be interested in helping us or at the very least be able to steer us in the right direction."

*****

Annie began her query, and she and Ed resumed a semblance of a normal life. Luke finally joined them for dinner one night. Annie made chicken with fennel, mashed potatoes and a tossed salad, and served it with homemade whole grain Irish soda bread and for dessert, a flourless chocolate torte.

Both Ed and Annie had hoped the comforting aspects of the meal and a more relaxed setting would encourage Luke to be more forthcoming about his life. He became animated when talking about the diving expedition he planned to participate in over the summer, but he changed the subject when Ed asked him about his experience with the SEALs. When questioned about his parents and siblings and about his social life, he responded, but only superficially. He said he planned to stay in Lighthouse Cove for another year or two but hoped he'd be able to find a position after that in a large metropolitan area. He also admitted that Emily's death had really shaken him, that he had never expected a crime so horrific to occur in this peaceful village. He helped them clean up, and after he left, Ed agreed with Annie that while he seemed a very nice young man, he appeared to be uncomfortable making small talk and was more introverted than either of them had expected.

Donna returned Annie's call and verified the story, as Angelica Hawthorn had told Ed, that the royals had been transporting jewels which hadn't been recovered. If, in fact, there was evidence they were buried under the museum she thought she might be able get some funding from sources in England to conduct the excavation if nothing surfaced in the States. The royal family and the citizens of the British Isles would be grateful for their return.

Chapter 46

Ed visited Charles in jail after learning that his trial was set for June. He appeared even paler and his tremors had increased since the last time the two had been together.

"Charles, I went to Toronto and spoke with Jennifer Ashwani, the current dean of your department at the university, and to Angelica Hawthorn and Pamela Huntsman. Jennifer gave me a copy of Thomas Battleforth's manuscript, and I learned about your ancestry. I now understand why, upon reflection, you might have changed your mind and decided to explore the possibility that the treasure might be buried in the museum's basement."

Charles looked down at the floor, averting his eyes from Ed.

"Finding the treasure would have righted a wrong done by one of your ancestors more than two centuries ago. But I don't understand why you didn't feel comfortable talking with Annie or the board about doing an exploratory excavation rather than taking the matter into your own hands."

Charles sighed and buried his head in his hands. "I don't know what you want me to say, Ed. I didn't want to tell anyone because I wasn't sure anyone would believe me. They may have thought it was just the ramblings of an old man trying to get some attention. I know you're trying to help, but I told you I'm guilty. I never wished Emily dead and am sick about that. It never should have happened, but my actions caused it. End of story."

"Well, this might make you happy," said Ed. "Annie called Donna Jones in England, and after she verified that the treasure was never found, Annie spoke with the museum board and your colleagues in Toronto. If there's any possibility the treasure is buried under the museum, they want to find it so they're going to try and obtain funding and get some archaeologists to volunteer their time to do an excavation on the site. I'll keep you posted. Please know how sorry I am things worked out the way they did. If you had called 911 the outcome of this would have been very different."

Later that day, Ed called Annie and told her about his conversation with Charles and the decline in his health. He wondered if Charles would live long enough to stand trial, let alone be alive to hear about the results of their query to obtain an excavation.

Chapter 47

Torrents of melting snow overflowed the curbs and gullies and rushed towards the lake during a sudden, unexpected thaw in February. A sunny, dry forecast for Valentine's Day encouraged Ed and Annie to call a group of friends and make reservations for dinner at the Bristol Harbor Grille.

The restaurant, perched on tree-trunk thick pilings, gleamed inside with bleached hardwood floors, a polished dark wooden bar at one end of the long, narrow room and square tables covered with crisp, white linen tablecloths at the other. For ambience and light, small glass harbor oil lamps served as centerpieces on each table, and the room was illuminated with these along with several nautical-themed wall sconces. Oversized windows surrounded three sides of the room, overlooking the marina, the harbor and beyond it, the lake.

As the group entered the restaurant, Annie spied Suzanne Gordon sitting at a four-top with her boyfriend, Garrett; a petite redheaded woman with hazel eyes; and an ivory-skinned woman with deep blue eyes and short, spiky black hair. Annie excused herself from their friends, followed by Ed, and went to greet Suzanne, who stood up and embraced her. As soon as the two women broke apart, Ed opened his arms and Suzanne walked into them.

"I'm so glad to see you, Suzanne." Ed, nodding to the others, smiled.

"You remember my friend, Garrett," Suzanne said as Garrett stood and shook hands with Ed and hugged Annie. She then introduced Garrett's law partner, Sheila Caldwell; and her spouse, Amy McBride, who was the pastry and dessert chef at Suzanne's father's restaurant.

"It's so nice to meet all of you," exclaimed Annie.

After a few more minutes of small talk, Ed remarked, "We don't want to take up any more of your time, so we'll let you get back to your dinner. Suzanne, now that we have our killer, I hope you'll be able to find some closure and put Emily's death in a less prominent place in your life."

"Thanks, Ed. I'm doing much better, but I'm very upset about Charles. I still can't believe he killed Emily. It just doesn't make sense."

"We all feel that way, but unfortunately his confession and the evidence seem to point to his guilt," countered Ed. "We're glad you're representing him, Garrett. At least we know he'll get a fair trial."

Garrett said, "I'm going to do my very best to make sure that Charles doesn't languish in jail for the rest of his life."

Annie smiled. "I certainly hope so. Now we do need to get back to our friends. Happy Valentine's Day."

Chapter 48

The balmy, spring-like weather continued to hold and after several days of sunshine, the grass, once spongy from the quick melt, dried and villagers rushed outdoors to take advantage of the mild sunny days. Because of the early snow and his involvement in Emily's murder investigation, Ed had not used his metal detector since November.

Instead of going to the beach, which was still soppy from the melted snow and ice, he awoke one bright morning and after quickly downing a cup of coffee threw on his hiking clothes and boots and with the detector in hand, headed to the village park where the museum stood.

Whatever he found he'd take to the police station, just in case someone had reported something missing. He'd donate anything left over that was in halfway decent condition to the annual firemen's spring flea market.

Just as he figured, his search yielded some coins, mostly pennies, some costume jewelry and a few other worthless trinkets, probably all lost during the past summer or fall when tourists and residents crowded the park for cookouts, concerts, festivals or to watch the sailboats gliding by on the lake.

He put some of the more valuable items in his pocket and tossed the rest in a small plastic trash bag he'd brought with him. As he headed out of the park towards his car, he noticed what looked at first like a credit card sticking up out of a pile of wet leaves and walked over to pick it up.

Upon further inspection, he recognized it as a drivers' license, displaying the photo of a young man. But he couldn't read the name on it because he'd left his reading glasses in his car when he'd donned his sunglasses.

Whoever this license belongs to probably has already reported it missing and filed for a duplicate, he thought to himself and started to throw it, along with his bag of trash, in a bin that was anchored next to a charcoal grill on the lawn. But then he changed his mind and decided to take it with him to the police station to see if anyone had called in and reported it missing.

At the station, after dumping everything he picked up in the park on the counter, he asked Rachel, the plump, bespectacled receptionist, to check and see if any of the objects had been reported lost over the past several months.

"Let me get the list," she said as she got up from her chair, pulling her cotton turtleneck sweater firmly down over her knit slacks. Now in her 50s, the cheerful brown-haired woman had worked at the station since graduating from high school. Since then, she'd married, borne two children and was now the proud grandmother of a baby boy.

While he was waiting for her to return, Ed looked more closely at the items on the counter and noticed a coin. It was the one he'd found on the beach the day of Emily's murder and had put in his pocket and forgotten. Picking it up off the counter and turning it over, he examined it closely. His eyes lit up. It was British, dated 1781, minted less than a decade before Thomas Battleforth landed on the beach at Lighthouse Cove. Excited at the discovery, he couldn't wait to show it to

Annie. It very well may have been one of Battleforth's, buried deep beneath the sand for generations.

Rachel returned with the list that she placed on the counter for the two of them to peruse. Nothing that had been reported missing was among the items Ed had unearthed, so he gathered up those he'd donate to the firehouse and threw the rest in a waste basket. He was walking out the door when he remembered the license.

"I'm having a senior moment," he said to Rachel, laughing. "I picked up a driver's license in the park. It's probably already been replaced, but let me get it out so you can check to see if anyone called in about it, just to make sure."

"What's the name on it?"

"I didn't have my glasses on so couldn't read the name," he answered, pulling his reading glasses out of his pocket. "Let's see who this belongs to."

Ed looked at the license, and astonishment registered on his face. "Well, well, what have we got here?" The name on the license was Michael Warren, address Ontario, NY.

"This can't be a coincidence. This must be the same Michael Warren I wanted to speak with who never responded to my email. I thought he might still be in South Korea, but apparently he's been living right under our noses," he said as Rachel looked quizzically at him. He quickly explained to her that the young man had been someone he'd wanted to talk with regarding Emily's murder.

"Is Chief Fisher back yet?" he asked Rachel.

"No. His mother's still hanging on, and he doesn't want to leave her. His father is not in terribly good shape either, so he needs to be there to look after him as well. Poor family. First Ellen's dad and now his mother. He's taken a leave of absence but thinks he'll be back in a couple of weeks."

"That's too bad. He's going through a tough spell, and I feel for him," remarked Ed.

"What about Carrie? Is she in?"

"She is. I'll buzz her and let her know you want to see her."

A minute later, sitting in Carrie's office, Ed showed her the coin.

"Wow, what a find!" she exclaimed. "This really could be another link to Thomas Battleforth and the possibility that the treasure is buried here. Annie's going to be beside herself when you give this to her."

"It is pretty exciting," Ed answered. "But I have something else to show you."

He took out the license and put it on Carrie's desk. "I'm wondering if this is the same Michael Warren I tried to contact who was part of the exploratory trip here with the folks from the University of Toronto."

"Luke's working with some techs on another horrible murder right now, but if you like, I can ask Brad to see what he can find out about the person on the license."

"Another murder? What's happened? Could it have anything to do with Emily's murder?"

"Not even remotely. I guess you haven't heard. A mother and daughter were found dead in their home early this morning. At first, it looked like a murder-suicide but there's some evidence that it may have been a double murder. There's apparently an estranged son/brother who has substance abuse problems who may be involved. The father died some years ago, and there's another daughter who lives out of state."

"How horrible for the surviving daughter. Maybe this will be easier to solve than the one we're working on."

"It's probably a bit more cut-and-dried. There's a BOLO out for the son."

"Well, since Luke is busy, I'd appreciate your asking Brad to see what he can dig up about this Michael Warren. Since we have an address, it may not be too lengthy a process or too difficult to verify whether he's the same person we're looking for. All we really need is to find out where he's working and his two or three previous addresses."

"I'll tell Brad to get on it right away, but there have to be hundreds of men living in the states with his name. What if this isn't the same Michael Warren?"

"I'm not going to worry about it. It's not worth spending too much time trying to track him down, but if he is living nearby it would be irresponsible of me to not follow up with him."

"I'll call you as soon as I hear anything," Carrie promised.

Some hours later, as Ed was pulling up to his garage, his cell phone rang. It was Carrie.

"I got the information you wanted about Michael Warren. I'm pretty sure he's the one you're looking for. He teaches English at the Wayne Central Middle School and got back last year after spending a couple of years teaching English as a second language in South Korea. His two previous addresses were in Toronto, where he attended the university, and in Ithaca, where he lived as a child. But something else popped up that might interest you. He applied for the duplicate license in November." Carrie paused. "A day after Emily's murder."

Ed pumped a fist. "That sheds a very different light on this. I wanted to talk with him to get any insights he might have had about Charles, but now that I know when he applied for the duplicate license, I'm wondering if he might be involved in the murder and was either in the building with Charles that night or if for some reason Charles is covering for him."

"I'm as excited as you are about this, but Ed, we've been that route before. Let's take this one step at a time," Carrie cautioned. "He might not be the person we're looking for, or if he is, he may have lost the license earlier in the fall and for some reason only realized it was missing the day after the murder. His applying for a duplicate when he did could be completely coincidental."

"Of course, it could. But I've been investigating murders for a long time and trust my instincts, Carrie, which are telling me that this Michael Warren knows something about Emily's murder."

"What's your plan?" Carrie asked.

"I'll go see Charles tomorrow and ask him some more questions. I'm hoping I can persuade him to tell me if they've been in regular contact. Then I'll pay a visit to Michael."

Chapter 49

Exotic spices and the smell of coconut wafted through the air as Ed walked into his house.

"I'm home," he called out to Annie, who appeared with a wooden spoon in hand, wearing an oversized white chef's apron.

"What's that wonderful smell?"

She smiled. "I'm experimenting. Al West, the chef on the cooking segment of this morning's news program on RNN made an Indian vegetable curry in a slow cooker that looked delicious. So that's what we're having tonight along with basmati rice, mango chutney and some Indian flatbread."

"Sounds delicious. How soon 'til dinner?"

"It's almost ready, but we have time for a drink before we eat. What would you like?"

"I'll have a scotch. What can I get for you?"

"There's an open bottle of sauvignon blanc in the refrigerator. I'll finish that up. Do you want a snack?"

"No, thanks. I don't want to ruin my appetite." Ed reached into his pocket and took out the coin and put it on the kitchen counter."

"What's this?" Annie asked.

"It's a coin I found in the sand the day of Emily's murder. Look at the date. I forgot I had put it in my pocket until today, when I pulled it out with other stuff I picked up at the park while I was metal detecting."

Annie took the coin in her hand and turned it over. Eyes widening, she started doing the happy dance. "This is great, Ed. I know there are other possibilities for why this coin was buried in the sand. There were settlers here during that time, although most of them weren't British, but this still makes Battleforth's story more credible. It may not be worth much monetarily, but along with the map, it would be part of an interesting exhibit."

Annie calmed down, and keeping with their nightly tradition, she and Ed—drinks in hand—sat side by side on chairs facing the fireplace in the living room and discussed their day, this time with Gretchen stretched out next to Annie on the floor. Annie's day had been uneventful, and she said she felt as though the museum was in good shape for its formal opening in a couple of months.

Ed told her about finding Michael Warren's driver's license; that he might be the same person who had been with the others on the trip from Canada, and his belief that Charles and Michael had been in the museum together when Emily was killed, and that Charles was covering for him.

"Oh, Ed," sighed Annie. "On one hand, I'm hoping that Michael's only involvement with this whole mess was as a reporter when he was a student at the university. I'd hate to find out there's any connection between him and Charles and the murder."

"I know, Annie," Ed interrupted. "This case has taken a very interesting turn."

"But," Annie continued, "on the other hand, I don't want Charles to be the killer. If Michael had anything to do with Emily's murder, then maybe Charles won't have to spend his remaining days in jail."

Ed responded that he planned to pay a visit to Charles the next day, and then, depending on the outcome of the interview, make a visit to Michael Warren.

Chapter 50

Ed was meeting his Navy buddies for lunch the next day so decided to wait until after that to visit Charles. The sky had turned gun-metal gray, and heavy, wet snow had begun to fall.

So much for an early thaw, thought Ed as he carefully drove five miles out of town to Phillips House, a restaurant located on a country road that meandered through acres of apple orchards. Stamping his feet in the toasty warm foyer to get the snow off his boots, he waved when he saw his friends and walked over to the table where they were sitting.

"Afternoon, guys, nice to see you," Ed said, as he slid into his chair. Cocking his head towards the window and the snow that had become increasingly heavier, he remarked, "One thing you can say about the weather around here is that if you're not happy with it, wait five minutes and it will change." Everyone laughed.

The server came over to the table and took their orders. The lunch special, a bowl of chili, garlic bread and a small side salad appealed to all the men, and settling in with their meals and beverages they chatted, catching up with each other.

George Wright and his wife had just had another grandchild; Bob Fergus and his wife had just returned from a Caribbean cruise; Larry Mandel, a widower, had met a lovely woman while taking an art appreciation class at the community college; and Jeff Ketchum told the group that after forty years of marriage he and his wife were divorcing, he'd bought a 45-foot sailboat and planned to sail from Lake Ontario to Manhattan in June with his new girlfriend, a thirty-year old financial planning consultant.

The group sat near the roaring fire that burned in the fireplace, and as he talked, Jeff commented on how warm the room was and peeled off his sweater revealing an open-collared blue oxford cloth shirt. The conversation shifted to Ed, and, of course, the murder. Ed caught the group up on Charles' arrest, trying in vain to change the subject as his friends pelted him with questions.

After several minutes, he had finally had enough and said, "Hey guys, can we move on to something else?"

They reluctantly agreed, and just as the conversation started to change, Ed noticed a pendant hanging around Jeff's neck, partially hidden by his shirt. It was a gold anchor. He recognized it, and then it hit him. Charles probably was covering for someone, but if not Michael Warren, Ed thought he knew who it was. He just couldn't figure out why.

Chapter 51

A guard led Charles, handcuffed, slouching, and dragging his feet, into the dimly lit interview room.

"Please take his cuffs off," Ed requested of the tall, muscular, uniformed guard. "He's no danger to me."

"Prison orders, sir. Sorry."

"Very well, but I'll be safe in here without you. I'll knock on the door when our conversation is finished."

The guard nodded and left the room.

"Good morning, Charles. How are you holding up?" Ed said kindly.

Charles breathed in and out rapidly, with a shaky sigh. "I'm doing fine, given my circumstances."

"Is your health worse?"

"My stamina's not too great, so mainly I sit quietly in my cell and read or watch TV. Sometimes I work in the library, and I'm teaching some inmates to read. They treat me well and are respectful, and I'm grateful for that."

"I want to help you, Charles. I'm here because I have reason to believe you didn't kill Emily."

"Ed, let's not go down that road again. I confessed, I'm guilty, and I'm prepared to suffer the consequences."

On his way to the jail, Ed remembered a conversation he'd had with Annie just after Emily's murder. He'd forgotten about it because what she told him didn't seem important at the time, but that one detail made a lie out of Charles' story about the sequence of events that happened that morning.

Ed revealed the conversation to Charles.

"When you gave your version of how you murdered Emily, you told us that you'd been in her office retrieving the map from a hidden drawer in her desk. But that's not true. The desk with the hidden drawer *had* been in Emily's office, but she needed more space for a filing cabinet, so she and Annie switched desks last September. Annie knew about the drawer because Donna had told her about it and once the desk was moved to her office, she found it and opened it. She assured me that there was nothing in it. No map, no papers." Charles looked startled.

"Yesterday I thought perhaps you were in the museum with another person, but now I believe you weren't there at all and that someone else may have killed Emily and you know who it is and are covering for him."

"You think I'm covering for someone?" sputtered Charles, caught completely off guard. "Why would you think that?"

"Because you're in ill health and figured you'd take the fall for the real killer."

"You know you can't prove that," Charles said evasively.

"I think I can. But what I don't understand is why you would want to cover for him. You can't know him all that well."

"I have no idea what you are talking about." Charles looked puzzled.

"Then let me explain it to you, Charles. Annie found something of his at the crime scene, although at the time when she told me I didn't recognize it or realize it was his. He was very wily at taking suspicion off himself. It's an anchor pendant that's part of a collection of jewelry available to retired and honorably discharged Navy officers, but more typically, it's worn by former Navy SEALs. I'm positive he was at the museum the night Emily was killed, so I ask again, why would you cover for Luke Callen?"

"Luke Callen?" Charles gasped. "I barely know Luke, and I'm not covering for him. I'm covering for someone else." Realizing what he'd just said, Charles cupped his hand in front of his mouth.

"Annie found Luke's anchor pendant on the floor in Emily's office," responded Ed patiently. "She gave it to him to take to the station, and he did, probably realizing that no one would suspect him, even if his prints were on it, because he had conveniently taken off his investigator's gloves. Later she found a chain, probably the one that broke off his neck during the struggle, when the pendant fell to the floor. How can you tell me you aren't covering for him? I believe he was there, but if you weren't with him, who was, and why is that person so important to you that you would go to jail for him?"

Charles stared at Ed but refused to answer.

Then it hit Ed and he knew. "Michael Warren? If it's not Luke, it must be Michael. Why would you do that?"

Charles put his head in his hands.

"Charles," Ed said sternly, "this charade has to stop. You weren't at the museum the night Emily was killed. I believe either Michael Warren or Luke Callen or both were there, I just don't know why. I will find out, so you might as well tell me what's really going on and what you know."

Charles shook his head. "I can't take this any longer. I wish you'd just go away and leave me alone."

"That's not going to happen, Charles. You didn't kill Emily, and I won't be party to putting you in jail for the rest of your life. If you say you don't know Luke I believe you, but the only other person you could possibly be protecting would be Michael Warren."

Charles remained silent.

"Charles, the only other lead we have is Luke, so you're leaving me no choice but to call Carrie and have her arrest him."

"That's not fair. You're mistaken about Luke; he's not involved. Despite what you think, the anchor and chain are most likely items we sell at the gift shop. I'm sure it's purely a coincidence that it looks like a piece of Navy jewelry."

"Then talk to me."

Charles sighed. "I can't let an innocent man go to jail, so you're leaving me no choice. It is Michael. Michael Warren."

"Why would you cover for Michael? From what I've been told, you barely know him. This isn't making any sense."

Charles moaned. "I'm covering for Michael because he's my son. There, now you know."

Shocked, Ed shook his head and thought, *Well, that's a new wrinkle to the case I never expected.*

Looking at Charles, he asked him why he'd never mentioned he had a son.

"I don't want to talk about this."

"You can't evade talking about this any longer, Charles. You've just admitted Michael is your son, so you might as well get the story out. My interrogation skills are pretty good, so if you don't tell me the truth, I'll get it from Michael."

"Please don't bother him. Michael's a decent young man. None of this is his fault. I didn't know until recently that he was my son. I had no idea when I met him at the university that we were related."

"You're convinced Michael had something to do with Emily's murder, aren't you?"

"Unfortunately, yes. I found something of his in the museum the morning of the murder. I confronted him, and the way he answered me made me believe he was at the museum at the time of her death."

"It sounds like we're going to be here awhile." Ed sighed. "Tell me what you know."

Chapter 52

Charles told Ed that he'd done research at Cornell one summer when he was in his early 50s and had met Liz Norman, a young, attractive librarian who worked at the graduate school of archaeology. They struck up what at first seemed to be a platonic friendship. She was about half his age, but Charles was attracted to her, and she later confessed that she felt attracted to him as well. They seemed to have a lot in common and started meeting after work, at first for coffee, then on weekends when they would take hikes together and sail on Seneca Lake in a boat he'd rented for the season, sometimes having drinks and dinner afterwards.

Several weeks after they met, they began an intimate relationship which for him had all the passion of the affair he'd had many years before with Angelica Hawthorn. He could hardly believe that after all those years he was finally in love again, and she seemed to return his feelings.

One evening late in August, before he went back to Toronto, Charles sailed with Liz along the lake to a hidden cove where they anchored. After sharing a simple meal, he proposed. Liz turned him down. She said she hadn't known him long enough to make that sort of commitment, and while she was pretty sure she loved him, she was convinced that because of their age difference it couldn't work as a permanent relationship. She didn't feel she was prepared to take care of him if he became ill as he aged or to become a young widow.

Charles said he argued with her, telling her that there are no guarantees, but she was resolute.

Early in their relationship, before they became lovers, Charles had told Liz that while he regretted not marrying, he'd accepted that he'd never father a child, and at his age it was probably for the best, because he thought he might be too set in his ways to be a good father. She used that as another reason for refusing his proposal, telling him she'd like to have children and despite his protestations to the contrary, she believed him when he first acknowledged that he probably wasn't father material.

She said that even if he had changed his mind, she didn't want to have children with someone who might not live to see them reach adulthood. Nothing he said could convince her otherwise. Devastated, Charles returned to Canada. He wrote and tried calling her, but she wouldn't speak with him. After several months he gave up, and they never saw one another again.

"Here I was, 50, and in love again. I thought I'd have a second chance, but once again that didn't happen. I finally resolved that marriage, and a permanent relationship with someone I loved, just wasn't in the cards for me. I got over her rejection, but I never forgot her."

He told Ed that after the hurting stopped he dated other women, had other affairs, but he never forgot Liz and became resigned to living his life alone.

Ed looked at Charles with compassion, thinking that despite his obvious intelligence and successful career, what a sad and tragic man he was.

"How did you find out about Michael?"

"By now you probably know a good bit of this story," Charles responded. "Michael majored in English at the University of Toronto. He interviewed me for a feature in the school newspaper and asked to accompany our team here to Lighthouse Cove. He expressed interest in a photo on my desk taken the summer I did research at Cornell, and when I told him about it, he talked about growing up in Ithaca and going fishing with his father. His last name was Warren, and the name wasn't a familiar one to me, so at the time I didn't think anything more about it."

"What happened next?"

"Nothing at first. We came here and decided it was a wild goose chase. Pamela and Angelica disagreed with our findings, but while disappointed, I trusted the opinions of our geologist and surveyor. Later, after I discovered I was related to the Merrill and Battleforth clans, I changed my mind."

"Did you see Michael after that?"

"No, not for a very long time. We had talked about going fishing, but Michael graduated and went to South Korea to teach for a couple of years, and I retired and moved here. We didn't keep in touch." Charles paused and took a deep breath.

"Then what happened?"

"He called me about a year ago. He *had* kept in touch with Pam Huntsman who'd mentioned in passing that I had retired to Lighthouse Cove. When he was hired as a teacher at the Wayne Central Middle School, he obtained my phone number from her. He called and told me he wanted to visit. I was delighted to hear from him and invited him to dinner."

"That apparently went well?"

"It did. I enjoyed his company, and we started spending more time together. There was a strong bond between us, and I felt as though Michael could have been the son I never had."

"When did you find out you were his father?"

"He had dinner with me one night, but he didn't tell me what he believed until the next day."

Charles continued, "As you know, I have several photos displayed on my mantel; many had been in my office at the university. He had asked me about them when he interviewed me, and that night said something about them again. He spent more than a few minutes looking at the one with Angelica and me and another that included him and the others that was taken just before we came here on our exploratory trip."

"Did you think that was strange?"

"Not really. Still, I said something to him about it, thinking that maybe he was taken with Angelica. She was quite beautiful. Michael agreed she was, but he seemed preoccupied and his response seemed lacking in sincerity. Then he remarked that he thought he looked a lot like I did when I was his age and pointed to both the photo with Angelica and me and the one with the two of us standing together in the group photo. I could certainly see a resemblance and made a stupid joke about it, telling him that maybe somewhere in the distant past we'd had ancestors in common. I never put two-and-two together."

Thinking about Michael's drivers' license photo and the one of the group on Charles' mantel, it hit Ed that Michael's observation was true. It just hadn't registered with him.

"Charles, didn't you see the resemblance between yourself and Michael?"

"Quite frankly, I never thought twice about it. After I found out he was my son I realized how much we do look alike."

"What happened next?"

"This is painful, Ed, and I'm not sure I want to talk with you more about this."

"At this point, Charles, I really don't think you have a choice."

Chapter 53

Charles took a deep breath:

"The next day we were fishing on the pier when Michael looked at me and said point blank that he thought I was his father. I was astounded and questioned him about why he would think that. He told me that until he was eight he grew up without a father. That's when his mother married David Warren who adopted him, but Michael wanted to know who his biological father was. When he questioned his mother, she was very evasive and wouldn't tell him. He needed his birth certificate for university, and no father was listed, so he resolved to search for him, despite his mother's objections.

"While helping his mother clear out the house before his parents moved to Chicago he found a box of photos, including one with her and a man he didn't recognize on a sailboat. He asked who the man was, and she said he had been a friend of hers but said that they'd lost touch and she didn't even remember why she'd kept the photo. He told me she took it from him, tore it up and tossed it. Her response bothered him, and he wondered if she were lying, but he decided to not press the issue and dropped the subject.

"Michael subsequently enrolled at the University of Toronto, and as you know, during his junior year he interviewed me and was quite taken by the photo on my credenza with me and my colleagues on our fishing trip. He later told me he recognized me. I was the same man in the photo he'd found in his parents' home, so he began putting the pieces of the puzzle together."

"Why didn't he say anything to you when he was still at the university?"

"He was scared to approach me because he wasn't sure how I would have responded. He had no real proof I was his father, just a strong suspicion. He said he'd thought about confronting his mother but was also afraid of her reaction and didn't want to open old wounds or cause a rift with her.

"When he was at my home and saw the photo of me with Angelica when I was about his age and then compared that to one with the two of us in the group photo, everything clicked."

Charles continued, "If I could turn back the clock there's so much I would have done differently. If I had known Liz was pregnant I would have been more persistent about her marrying me, or at the very least I would have insisted on helping to support Michael. I would have been a presence in his life. She never gave me a chance. And despite being resigned to never having children, I would have loved Michael. I love him now.

"Michael admitted that Liz has been a loving parent, the marriage has been a happy one, and David's been a good father. But he was and still is very angry his mother never told him about me."

"Did he think you were in some way responsible for his not knowing?"

"He assumed I'd walked out on his mother when I found out she was pregnant, which is why she refused to tell him anything about the man in the photo. I didn't want to cast blame on Liz but couldn't let him believe that, so I told him the truth, that when I left Ithaca to return to Toronto I had no idea Liz was pregnant and that she never contacted me. I offered to take a paternity test, and if in fact it proved I was his father, I promised him I'd start acting like one."

Grief-stricken over the conversation and determined to make things right, with Michael's concurrence Charles took the test and learned he was his son. He suggested that Michael let his mother know about his finding Charles, but angry and resentful, Michael refused. Charles told Ed that he still wasn't sure Liz knew what Michael had discovered, but he decided to not get in the middle of it.

"Michael has been unable to get past his childhood, Ed, and I'm not sure why. He grew up with a loving mother and a father who considered him his own. Even 25 years ago there wasn't much of a stigma about having a child out of wedlock, especially in Ithaca—it's a progressive university town. I can't imagine he was teased in school, lots of children grow up in single parent homes. He must have missed having a dad terribly when he was a small boy, but wounds like that can heal. For some reason, he's unable to move past this or his anger at Liz."

"We're back to the original reason for my visit, Charles," stated Ed. "Annie and Carrie have never believed you killed Emily, and you've admitted you weren't at the museum at the time of the murder but found something belonging to Michael after the fact that led you to believe he was there."

"At this point, Ed, I still plan to stick with my story. I've signed a confession, and I won't let my defense lawyer call you to testify against me. No one needs to know. Please let me do this," he pleaded.

Exasperated, Ed explained, "I can't. Ethically and legally I'm obligated to report our conversation.

"Your guilt at not being present in Michael's life is clouding your judgment, Charles. Shielding him is only going to make things worse. It's been proven that there's a strong likelihood that if someone gets away with murder once, they may likely kill again. Who will be next? So, I'm asking you once more, why do you believe Michael killed Emily?"

Charles hung his head. "He never confessed, but I found his scarf on the floor in the museum the morning of the murder."

"Excuse me?"

"This past October I gave Michael a cashmere scarf for his birthday that I'd purchased during a trip I took to England last August. The colors are distinctive. They're the colors of the Merrill family crest: tan, red, blue and silver. I had his initials monogrammed on it, plus there's a small label in one corner identifying the shop where I purchased it."

"When I came into the museum before the meeting and saw the disarray, one of the first things I noticed was his scarf on the floor near the door. At first, I thought maybe he'd recently taken a tour of the museum and lost it then, but I remembered him telling me he'd taken a tour shortly after he moved here, which was during the summer and before I knew he was my son. I don't believe he'd have any reason to return unless he had something to do with the break-in and the possible disappearance of Emily. I didn't know at the time that she'd been murdered, but I took the scarf and stuffed it into my briefcase, just in case he was involved in the burglary.

"I called him as soon as I found it, before Chief Fisher arrived. He had already started work so didn't pick up. I left a message for him to call me as soon as possible, but he didn't call me back until he got home from school. I told him I had found his scarf and confronted him about his whereabouts early that morning. He sounded relieved that I'd found the scarf but refused to admit he'd been at the museum. He said he knew he'd misplaced it but had no idea why I found it there. I knew he was lying."

"Why do you think he would have gone to the museum that morning, Charles?"

"While misguided, he may have thought it would bring the two of us closer if he found the treasure. I can certainly understand that; he knows about my ancestry. Perhaps he decided to go into the museum and do a little exploring to see if he could find the location where he believed the treasure was buried, maybe even begin to dig for the box, but got interrupted when Emily came in early and there was a scuffle resulting in her death."

"You found his scarf, but how did he get into the museum? You, Annie and Suzanne were the only ones with keys. Did you give him one?"

"No. I did not. I have no idea how he got in unless he knows how to pick a lock, and I'd be very surprised if he did. Despite the trouble he's in, he's a nice young man, Ed, and none of this would have happened if he'd known from birth that I was his father. Please let me take the fall for him."

"You were not derelict in your duty as a father, Charles, and it's not your fault that his mother refused to tell him anything about you. If Michael killed Emily, he's the one who needs to face the consequences of his actions and be punished for it."

"What are you going to do?"

"First, I'm going to call Carrie and tell her about our conversation. I expect she will get in touch with the DA to inform him about your false confession and suspicion that Michael was involved in Emily's murder. Then I plan to drive to Michael's house to interview him. If he confesses or we find enough evidence to indicate his involvement, we'll arrest and charge him for Emily's murder. I'm also going to talk with Luke Callen because, despite your protestations, I believe he may have been an accomplice, although I have no idea why. While charges will be dropped against you for the murder, there may be more jail time in your future for purposely withholding evidence."

After talking with the guard about his conversation with Charles and requesting he not be given access to a telephone so that he couldn't call Michael to give him a heads up, Ed left the prison convinced of Michael and Luke Callen's involvement in Emily's death. As a retired Navy SEAL, Luke would have had access to the same collection of jewelry that his friend, Jeff, did, and Ed was positive that the anchor with the initials LC belonged to him, rather than inscribed on a Lighthouse Cove pendant sold at the museum gift shop. Plus, Annie had found that broken chain she couldn't identify. By now it was late afternoon, and since Michael was a teacher, Ed hoped he'd be home. When he arrived, Michael was just putting the key in his lock. Ed intercepted him.

Chapter 54

"Michael, my name is Ed DeCleryk."

"I know who you are."

"May I come in? I'd like to talk with you."

"What about?"

"C'mon, Michael, you know why I'm here. I just came from a visit with Charles Merrill, who told me he's your biological father. He admitted under great pressure that he didn't kill Emily Bradford and believes you may have been involved in her death. Now, may I come inside, or do we have to discuss this at the police station?"

Without a word, Michael opened the door and motioned for Ed to precede him. Ed entered and looked around. The small gray vinyl-sided townhouse was simply furnished with pieces from big box stores and flea markets. Books crammed freestanding shelves in the living room, and Michael had converted the dining room into an office. Michael sat on the sofa and Ed in a large chair facing it in the small living room.

"I'm going to be very blunt, Michael. I'm relatively sure you killed Emily Bradford, probably with an accomplice. I'm fully able to understand that her death may have been accidental, but I don't understand why you didn't call the police or 911 when she fell. You wouldn't be nearly in the amount of trouble you are now. I'm also baffled about why you'd let your dad take the fall for you. Unless you were acting, from what he told me it sounds like you and Charles have forged a pretty solid bond."

The wiry young man, as Ed had observed, did indeed look like his father when he was in his 20s. Of medium height, he had light hair, pale blue eyes, a square, dimpled jaw and a trim, athletic figure. In a flash, Ed recognized Michael as the solitary figure dressed in black at Emily's funeral.

"You were at Emily's funeral, weren't you? You were the one standing in the background, dressed in black."

Michael started to cry. "It was all a horrible mistake. I never meant for this to happen."

"But you did let it happen, and even worse, you let your father, an ill, elderly man, make a false confession to save your own hide. That's reprehensible."

"I had no choice," Michael insisted, tears streaming down his cheeks. "My dad found my scarf at the scene and confronted me. He assumed I'd killed Emily but, because I denied it, wasn't completely certain. After your wife gave him the map she'd found in the basement, he called me. He said he was sure I was Emily's killer because I was one of only a few who had a copy of the map and had reason to be in the basement the morning she died. He said he was going to confess to protect me. I protested, but he threatened that if I came forth and admitted the truth, he'd accuse me of lying and everyone would believe him. I didn't kill Ms. Bradford and wouldn't confess to something I didn't do, but I couldn't tell him what really happened that morning."

"I'm confused. If you didn't kill Emily, why couldn't you tell him what happened?"

Michael was quiet for a few seconds. "I was there, but I did not kill Emily Bradford. I'm tired of living with all these lies and my guilt at not coming forward after she was murdered. If I tell you who did kill her, I'm putting others at risk. If you want a confession I'll give you one, but others will be harmed. Go ahead. Arrest me," he said, his demeanor changing from being contrite to belligerent.

"Wait a minute. You just said you didn't kill her, but you're willing to take the fall for someone else? After your dad took the fall for you? What the hell is going on here? Has someone threatened you? Are you being blackmailed? I think I know who you're protecting, but why?"

Michael looked away from Ed and refused to answer.

"Michael, this must end. Who was with you the night Emily was killed?"

The young man sat quietly with his hands in his lap, looking stoically at Ed.

"Okay, then *I'll* tell you," said Ed, giving him a steely look. "I have good reason to believe that the person with you on the morning of Emily's death was Luke Callen. There's strong evidence implicating him in her murder. So, what I'm going to do right now is call the police station and have Luke arrested and escort you there where we will put both of you in a room together and question you. We will not leave until we have the truth, and believe me, by the end of today, regardless of your stubbornness, we will get it," replied Ed, who by now had lost all patience.

Michael's sighed, his breath raspy. "I'm not holding out on you because of myself. It's because of Charles, my dad. If I confess, he'll be in danger."

"What?"

He sat quietly and refused further comment.

"Michael, did Luke threaten to hurt Charles if you came forth and told the police what happened? We can protect him, especially with Luke in custody, but you must tell me what happened that morning. Why would the two of you be in the museum, and why is Emily dead?"

Chapter 55

Michael took a deep breath and began talking. He explained that he'd obtained a copy of Battleforth's manuscript and the map just before he interviewed Charles for the newspaper article. He'd filed them as keepsakes, but after Charles confirmed he was his father, decided to do some research about the HMS Orion and shipwrecks off the coast of Lighthouse Cove. If the team had missed something and the treasure really might be buried in the museum, he reasoned that if he could find evidence of it, it would be a way to forge a closer bond with Charles.

He discovered a special interest group about shipwrecks on Lake Ontario on Facebook and started a conversation with someone whose chat name was Sea Lion. Sea Lion had joined the group after reading a brochure about the history of Lighthouse Cove that included information about shipwrecks on the lake.

They became online friends and after discovering they both lived in the same county in upstate New York, decided to meet for coffee. They hit it off, and Michael showed Sea Lion the map and gave him his copy of Battleforth's manuscript. Sea Lion was, of course, Luke Callen.

After reading the manuscript, Luke called Michael and they agreed to meet again. They both believed the treasure could be buried in the museum, and Luke offered forth the argument that since Thomas Battleforth had used a rock, it probably wasn't buried too deeply. A formal excavation might not be necessary.

Michael said that when he was at the university he had done some research for the story he was writing about Charles and learned it was possible to do a small archaeological excavation using a trowel and spade. He suggested to Luke that they talk with Charles to try and convince him to help, or to the museum director, Annie DeCleryk. Luke was adamant that he didn't want to get anyone else involved, and Michael capitulated.

Shortly after he moved to the area, Michael had taken a tour of the museum, but when he asked about the basement the docent said it was off limits and only used for storage. He and Luke hatched a plan to go into the museum one night, but they weren't sure how to get in. Luke knew that if the two were discovered he could lose his job, but he seemed to like the idea of taking a risk and convinced Michael that they could go forth with the plan without getting caught.

Michael and Luke agreed that if they did find the copper box with anything in it, they would find a way to explain its discovery so whatever was in it could be returned to England. At first Luke argued that if there were some small items that didn't seem valuable, maybe they could keep them as mementos, souvenirs for their efforts. Michael strongly objected, and Luke backed off but promised to continue working with Michael to find the treasure.

Michael told Ed that Charles had once volunteered that he, Annie and someone named Suzanne were the only ones with keys to the museum. He knew Charles color-coded his keys and kept them on a ring that he placed, when not in use, in a dish on the small credenza just inside his front door. One night while they were having dinner, Michael expressed curiosity about the keys on Charles' key ring, and what the colors meant.

Charles told him about each key and pointed out the one to the museum, which was coded with a blue dot.

Several days later, he visited Charles to watch a ballgame with him, and before the game started they decided to order a pizza. Michael, a long-distance cyclist, had ridden his bike to Charles' house, so Charles gave him his set of keys and told him to use his car to pick up the pizza. Seizing what he saw was a perfect opportunity, he stopped at the hardware store on his way to the pizza parlor and had a copy of the museum key made.

Luke lived in a rented beach cottage within walking distance to the museum. About 5:00 the morning of the murder, Michael drove to his cottage, parked his car, and carrying a small trowel and spade, walked with him to the museum. The pair had chosen the early hour because it was still dark and would also give them enough time to explore without Michael being late for work. Luke had worked late the night before so wasn't expected at the police station until mid-morning.

Using the key, they entered the museum, went downstairs and with a low-watt flashlight shining on the spot they started digging, keeping their gloves on because the basement was so cold. When they heard a noise upstairs they thought it might be an intruder, so they quickly grabbed two boxes from the shelves, put them over the hole and placed the map between them for safe keeping, planning to go back downstairs to continue their digging after they found out what the noise was.

Whispering for Michael to stay behind, Luke grabbed a coal scuttle that was lying next to the old coal furnace and crept up the steps. Emily saw him as he surfaced from the basement but didn't recognize him and started screaming. He tried to quiet her, telling her he could explain why he was there, but she panicked and started to run out of her office to the front door. In Michael's words, his friend "freaked out," and started screaming at Emily to shut up or he would make her shut up.

By now, Michael had crept upstairs to see what was going on, and that's when he saw Luke hit Emily with the scuttle. She went down, and Michael thought he'd killed her, but she wasn't dead. He wanted to call 911. Luke told him that wasn't going to happen. If they ever wanted to get out of this, Emily couldn't live because she could identify them, and he wasn't going to lose his job because of her. Michael said Luke was completely out of control.

Ignoring Michael's protests, Luke picked up Emily's unconscious body, carried it across the lawn and threw her over the bluff. Michael tried stopping him on his way out the door and said that's probably when his scarf fell. When he got to school that morning, he realized it was missing but hoped it had fallen off in the school parking lot until his dad called. He'd spent the first few months after Emily's death paralyzed with fear and anxiety but somehow managed to go about his daily routine and continue teaching. The entire incident eventually became surreal for him and receded from being ever present.

"That's quite a story, Michael, but what if Emily hadn't been there and you actually did find the box with the treasure? How would you have explained finding it without implicating yourselves in the break-in?"

"That's easy. We would have filled the hole, put the boxes back and then a few days later, we would have said we'd found it on the beach when the water had receded."

"I understand why your father confessed. He wanted to protect you. But if you'd called 911, Emily would still be alive, her fall would have been deemed an accident, and you wouldn't be facing a murder charge. You would have been arrested for breaking and entering, and since it probably was a first offense you may have gotten off with probation or a fine and suspended sentence since nothing was stolen."

Michael wiped his nose and sniffed. "Luke's career would have been ruined, and probably mine as well. I'm a teacher, and there's no way I would have been able to keep my job. I told you. I wanted to call 911. I even got my cell phone out to make that call. That's when Luke threatened me. I knew what he did for a living, and he used that as leverage against me. He was acting crazy and not at all like the man whom I'd met for coffee to talk about shipwrecks. I was terrified."

"How did he threaten you, Michael?"

"He said he knew how to plant evidence that would convincingly make it seem like I had broken into the museum and killed Emily, and that if I reached for my phone, *he* would call 911 and tell the dispatcher that during an early morning run he'd seen lights on in the museum and then someone carrying a body and throwing it over the bluff. He'd say he'd called out to the perpetrator, meaning me, to stop, but that I'd started to flee, and because he always carried a gun for protection when he jogged before daylight, he'd shot a warning shot into the air. When I continued to run he'd say he shot again, but I dodged and turned around and the bullet hit an artery in my neck, killing me. He told me he'd appear very remorseful. There would be an investigation, of course, but he knew his story would hold up because of who he was. Everyone would believe that I'd broken into the museum and killed Emily. He warned me if I said anything about the truth of what happened, ever, he'd not only find a way to kill me, but also go after my dad."

"I wanted to confess and promised I wouldn't mention he was with me, but Luke said neither of us could be implicated in the crime and he knew I'd cave under questioning. Look at what's happening now."

Ed asked, "Michael, was Luke wearing a pendant with an anchor?"

"He was. Before he hit Emily, he grabbed her, and when she tried to pull away, she grabbed at his shirt. The chain broke, but I don't think he realized it. He was in such a hurry to get her body out to the bluff that I think he forgot about it. He told me to trash the building and make it look like a burglary, and when he came back he said we needed to get out of there, so we ran. By then it was snowing heavily and was just starting to get light. I was almost late for work.

"I don't care so much about myself, my life is probably over anyway. But I would not have been able to live with my guilt if Luke went after my dad. He's had enough to deal with, with his failing health. I know he isn't going to live much longer, but I couldn't have his murder on my conscience."

"I promise you, Michael, Luke will soon be in custody for Emily's murder. He's not going to hurt your dad."

"There's more I haven't told you. Once my dad confessed, Luke phoned me. He said he knew I'd be tempted to come forward and tell the truth to get my dad out of jail, but that there was one other person he'd go after if I did that."

"And who was that?"

Michael hesitated before responding, then said quietly, "Annie. Your wife. He said she'd been nice to him and he liked her, but if I said anything ever, to anyone, he'd make sure she had a tragic accident, perhaps a fall down the cellar steps at the museum since the two of them spent time alone there. I never met her, but I saw her once, at Emily's funeral. She has kind eyes. I couldn't let there be another murder at the museum."

"He threatened to kill Annie? My wife? Ed was horrified. "She befriended him, for God's sake!"

Chapter 56

Ed picked up his phone and called Carrie. He told her he was arresting Michael Warren as an accessory to Emily's murder. He'd confessed that Luke had been with him and was the one who had killed her. "Have you seen him today?"

"Oh darn, he was just in. He arrested the man I told you about in the double homicide. I gave him an update on the case and told him you'd gone to talk with Charles and were then going to find Michael to question him. I said that we pretty much figured out that Michael had probably killed Emily. He looked surprised and then concerned and left my office in a big hurry. I was a bit perplexed about his reaction, but after I thought more about it I assumed that maybe what I told him triggered something about this other murder case."

"How long ago was that?"

"Just a few minutes ago."

"Carrie, I need you to do something for me. Quickly. I'll give you the full details later, but Luke's threatened to kill Annie." Carrie gasped, and Ed looked at his watch.

"Annie takes a late afternoon yoga class on Thursdays. She should be at Suzanne's studio right now. Luke probably doesn't know that, so she's likely still safe. Please ask Brad to go to the studio and keep her and the other students there under guard until we capture Luke. Tell Brad to not let anyone leave. And find Luke and arrest him for murder. He may be on his way to our house."

Carrie spoke with Brad who hurried out of the police station and rushed across the street to Suzanne's studio, explaining to the class that someone in addition to Charles Merrill had surfaced as a suspect in Emily Bradford's murder and was on the loose, and he couldn't let them out of the building until he was apprehended. Suzanne and the students were bewildered and frightened, but Brad had been advised to not give much detail.

In the meantime, Carrie ran to her squad car, and sirens blazing, headed for the DeCleryk's house where she found Luke walking up their driveway.

"Stay very still, Luke, and turn around."

Luke feigned surprise. "What's this about, Chief? I was just coming to see Annie," he said innocently.

"Game's up. I only know the sketchy details, but I know you murdered Emily Bradford and that you threatened to kill Michael Warren, Charles Merrill and Annie. You're going to go away for a very long time." Luke looked straight at Carrie and pulled out his gun.

"Put the gun down, Luke. Shooting me won't accomplish anything. You can't get away with this."

Before she could retrieve it from him, he placed his gun against his temple and whispered, "I'm sorry."

"Luke, move your gun away from your head and put it on the ground. I don't believe you really want to die. You don't have to hurt yourself or anyone else. Please, do as I say."

"None of this should have happened," Luke said, distraught. "I didn't mean for it to happen. When Emily started screaming, all I wanted was for her to stop. She looked like a woman I killed when I was in Afghanistan and when she screamed, I started remembering it all over again. When the newscasters announced her name as the victim of the murder a couple of days later, I couldn't believe I really had killed her. I lost control, but I didn't mean to. I can't take it anymore, I can't seem to stop remembering what happened in Afghanistan."

"Luke, listen to me. We can sort this out. Don't do this to your family or those of us here in Lighthouse Cove who care about you. We can get you help. It's over."

His eyes looking wild and unfocused, Luke laid his gun on the ground, walked toward Carrie and put his hands in the air.

Carrie handcuffed Luke, guided him into the squad car, locked the door and then retrieved his gun, emptying the bullets into her pocket.

When she returned, she said, "You're under arrest for the murder of Emily Bradford and for threats against Charles Merrill, Michael Warren and Annie DeCleryk." She read him his rights. By now, he was surprisingly compliant and docile.

Chapter 57

Later that afternoon, after Luke and Michael were in custody, Ed, Carrie, and Annie met for a drink at The Brewery. Annie, shaken and very sad, nursed a white wine, Ed drank scotch, neat, and Carrie drank a ginger ale.

"When did you guess it was Luke, Ed?" asked Carrie.

"I suspected he was involved when I had lunch with my Navy buddies. All along, the anchor bothered me. I knew I'd seen one like it before but couldn't remember where. Then, when I saw it on my friend Jeff, it hit me. The initials didn't stand for Lighthouse Cove, they stood for Luke Callen. The pendant was a piece of Navy jewelry. I've never been into that stuff, but Jeff's worn his pendant for years. It wasn't, as Annie thought, something from the museum gift shop."

"I was completely fooled," stated Annie, tears welling up in her eyes. "I thought he was so sweet, and he seemed to like me. I can't help feeling a bit guilty. If I hadn't given him a copy of the brochure I wrote on the history of Lighthouse Cove none of this would have happened. He only became interested in the lost treasure when he read about it."

"Annie, you can't beat yourself up over this," Ed responded. "Someone who is emotionally healthy would never have read your brochure and then spiraled out of control just to find the treasure. You had no way of knowing what he would do."

She shook her head and wiped tears from her eyes.

246 Murder in the Museum

"Luke *does* like you, Annie," Carrie said. "When I got him to the station, he said that he only used your name to scare Michael into keeping quiet. He said you'd always been kind to him, and he never would have hurt you. He cried."

"Then why did he come to our house?"

"He said he was coming to see you, but not to hurt you. He told me he knew after I told him that Ed had met with Charles and was meeting with Michael that Michael would cave under pressure and tell Ed what happened, and he'd probably be arrested. He wanted to tell you in person and apologize to you. Then he was going to kill himself."

"Do you believe him?" Annie asked.

"I do. And I believe the rest of what he told me, too."

She continued, "He said the entire situation got miserably out of control. He admitted to blackmailing Michael but insisted Emily's death was an accident. He told me a terrible story about something that happened when he was in Afghanistan. He said he was part of a covert operation to eliminate a terror cell in a remote village there. His squad had been given the information of their location by a confidential informant, indicating that to his knowledge there were no civilians in the area."

"Have you verified his story?" Ed asked.

"Yes. He gave me the name and contact info of his CO who at first didn't want to speak with me, but after I told him what had happened he hung up, got clearance and called me back and admitted that what Luke told me about his time in Afghanistan actually occurred."

"I can only imagine what happened next," remarked Annie, still sniffling.

"It's truly horrible, Annie. It was dusk, and when they got there, weapons unconcealed and poised to strike, there was a woman walking past the doorway of the building where they suspected the terrorists were hiding. When she saw them she froze, started screaming and reached behind her back to grab something. She was wearing a black hijab, and a black long-sleeved blouse and long black skirt, and she had what they thought was a backpack strapped to her back. They could see the wide straps over her arms. They thought she either had a grenade in it or was a suicide bomber getting ready to set it off. To stop her, Luke shot her right between the eyes. She fell backward, dead. The insurgents came out of the building and there was a gunfight, and the SEALs killed everyone."

Ed said, "What a harrowing story. It's mind-boggling what our military personnel have to deal with over there."

"There's more," continued Carrie. "After the SEALs were sure everyone was dead, they started looking at the bodies, just to make sure there were no explosives on them, and to see if they had any sort of identification. Luke, who also had some training with a bomb squad, went to the dead woman and turned her over, planning to disable the bomb or grenade if he found one. What he found instead was a baby-pack with a dead baby, probably not more than a few months old. When his mother fell on her back after being shot, she smothered him."

Tears welled up in Carrie's eyes, and Annie started crying again. Annie said, "How devastating. That poor woman and her family. Poor baby. And poor Luke. How would he have known that, and how could he have ever recovered from what he'd done? His guilt must be overwhelming."

"He couldn't," continued Carrie, after taking a deep breath and wiping her eyes. "The informant gave the SEALs incorrect information about there being no civilians in the area. An investigation indicated that the woman had merely been at the wrong place at the wrong time. She lived in a nearby compound and was walking past the building on her way to her sister's house when she saw the SEALs approaching. She must have been scared witless, screamed, and put her hand behind her to instinctively protect her child. Luke was cleared of any wrong doing, but what he had done weighed heavily on him."

"And he, of course, felt huge remorse and was diagnosed with PTSD as the result of the incident," remarked Ed.

"Yes. But it wasn't so bad that he couldn't function. The doctor he saw recommended he be honorably discharged, believing that after serving several tours of duty in the Gulf one more incident probably *would* drive him over the edge, so he left the service.

"He went back to Connecticut and lived with his parents, got counseling and then after getting clearance from the psychiatrist he was working with, decided to go into law enforcement and got a masters' degree in criminal justice from the University of New Haven. No one he talked with thought he'd be a risk or have a relapse."

"Then why did he react the way he did to Emily?" Annie asked.

Carrie continued, "He said that for some reason his PTSD symptoms had recently returned. He was having flashbacks. Loud noises startled him. He'd been jumpy and making bad decisions and taking unnecessary risks. He said he hadn't been sleeping well, and his nightmares had returned, so he started self-medicating by drinking heavily in the evenings, hoping alcohol would help him. After he got home from Captain Rick's after his shift ended that night he continued to drink."

"He told me he'd had a flashback of what happened in Afghanistan after Emily started screaming. She reminded him of the woman he killed. Like Emily, she was small with green eyes." Carrie took a sip of her drink and picked at a piece of popcorn.

"I am without words to describe my sadness," stated Annie, blowing her nose. "What a trying and upsetting day, and what a tragedy all around."

She paused for a second. "I've noticed you're drinking ginger ale. Aren't you feeling well? I know this was a tough day for you. Is your stomach bothering you?"

"I feel physically fine, Annie, at least late in the afternoon I do. Right now, emotionally not so much. Morning's the tough time, though. I was going to wait a bit to tell you, but now is as good a time as any, especially after telling you about Luke. We could all use some happy news. Matt and I are going to have a baby."

Annie squealed, jumped up and hugged Carrie, who in turn hugged Ed.

"What a great way to end an otherwise horrible day," grinned Ed, raising his glass in a toast.

Chapter 58

Luke was arraigned and charged with first-degree burglary and second-degree murder. With his concurrence, his attorney, Sheila Caldwell, and the district attorney worked out a deal with the judge's approval. Instead of bail, he would spend the months prior to the trial in a secure psychiatric prison facility to receive treatment for the recurring PTSD.

At the trial, Sheila let Luke testify, feeling that if the jury heard his story and saw how truly remorseful he was about what he'd done, they might be inclined to acquit him because of extenuating circumstances. But the prosecuting attorney, upon cross-examination, also got him to admit that while his judgment had been impaired because of the PTSD, he'd purposely committed the burglary, understood Emily's death was not an accident as he had earlier stated, and that by throwing her body off the cliff he was condemning her to death. He admitted he knew that blackmailing Michael was a way to avoid facing the consequences of his actions, but stated that despite threatening to shoot him, he had not been carrying a gun that morning.

Before taking the stand, he sat quietly, his head down and eyes bleak. During the cross-examination he cried, but the jury, while sympathetic and believing he was truly contrite, was still convinced that Emily could have been saved if Luke had allowed Michael to call 911 and found him guilty on both charges.

Luke's parents and siblings had traveled from Connecticut and spent the duration of the brief trial at a local inn. During the sentencing phase, they asked for leniency, stating mitigating factors including his heartfelt remorse, stellar military career, the horrific murder in Afghanistan he'd unwittingly committed, and the fact that, other than in the line of duty, he'd never killed anyone nor had a criminal record.

Jon Bradford's family sat through the trial, and initially forgiving and empathetic, had been prepared to join Luke's family in asking for leniency. But after learning he'd been aware that when he threw Emily off the bluff she would die, and how he'd blackmailed Michael and threatened the lives of Charles and Annie, they declined to speak.

Before sentencing, Luke stood. Turning towards the Bradford family, he apologized and asked for their forgiveness. Annie, who had sat through the trial, was present in court that day, and he faced her and told her he never would have hurt her and regretted causing her any distress.

Impressed with his genuine remorse and his parents' heartfelt pleas, Judge Tyler nevertheless rebuked Luke for not seeking professional help for the PTSD when the symptoms had recurred. She acknowledged that while his career as a detective might have been over, he most likely could have remained in law enforcement in some capacity, given his credentials.

She said she appreciated the sacrifice he'd made during his service as a Navy SEAL and was sympathetic about what he had endured in Afghanistan, but by admitting knowing right from wrong, he must have also understood that if he had faced up to his problems and sought treatment, Emily would still be alive.

She gave him credit for the time he'd already served and sentenced him to the minimum allowed by New York state law, a total of fifteen years for the murder, three years for the burglary, to be served concurrently. In prison, he would continue to receive counseling for the PTSD, with eligibility for parole after fifteen years.

Charles was charged with falsifying his confession and tampering and withholding of evidence. Not wanting a trial, he pleaded guilty. His attorney, Garrett Rosenfeld, also asked for leniency, indicating that although misguided, he had been trying to protect his son. Rosenfeld also reminded the court that Charles was ill and not likely to survive a prison sentence. The judge agreed and fined him $1,000 but gave him his freedom for time served and for his cooperation.

Michael was charged with third-degree burglary and second-degree murder. Because he'd been traumatized and threatened by Luke and had agreed to testify against him, his attorney successfully negotiated a plea deal to get the murder charge expunged. He surrendered his passport and was released on his own recognizance after Charles paid his $5,000 bail. Frightened and remorseful, he asked Charles to contact his parents because he couldn't bring himself to make the call. Charles spoke with them, explained everything that had happened, and met them at the airport in Rochester when they flew in the next day. Liz and Charles made their peace with one another, and with support from her husband, David, committed to ongoing contact for Michael's sake.

Ignoring advice from his attorney, Damon Weathers, Michael decided at the last minute to plead guilty. He, too, wanted to avoid a trial. The judge, while cognizant of his clean record and fear for his life and the lives of his father and Annie, admonished him for his lack of judgment in committing the burglary. He was fined $500, sentenced to six months in prison, where he spent his time teaching reading to illiterate inmates, and after that to five years' probation. As expected, he lost his teaching job, but after he was released secured a position working at a housing project teaching English to immigrant residents. Weekends, he continued as a volunteer at the prison.

An accomplished writer, he decided to apply for a position in the Master of Arts creative writing program at the University of Rochester. He was accepted, Charles paid for his education, and with Michael's parents created a scholarship fund for that department in Emily's name.

Working with Annie, Donna Jones obtained a grant from a foundation in England to conduct a professional excavation in the basement of the museum, using experienced archaeologists from the University of Toronto and Cornell University. By then, Charles had moved to a condo in Toronto and transferred the deed from his house in Lighthouse Cove to Michael. His health somewhat improved since Emily's murder had been solved, he came back to observe the excavation, but as his team had originally concluded, it yielded no king's treasure.

Chapter 59

On a sun-dappled Saturday afternoon in mid-November, just short of a year after Emily's murder at the museum, Suzanne feted Emily's friends and relatives at a memorial picnic in her backyard. Oaks and maples that just a few weeks before had been ablaze with brilliant color stood sentry, their sturdy trunks framed beneath a bright azure sky. The white-capped sapphire bay, now devoid of the motor and sailboats that earlier in the month had been pulled up from the water and securely stowed away in boat houses and storage facilities, gently lapped against the seawall behind the cottage.

Aromatic cherry logs crackled in fire pits that ringed the leaf-strewn lawn, providing warmth against the crisp autumn air. Attending the picnic were Ed and Annie; Carrie, Matt and their newborn daughter, Natalia; Ben and Ellen Fisher; Suzanne's friend, Garrett Rosenfeld; Sheila Caldwell and her spouse, Amy; Jon Bradford and his family; members of the museum board and some of Emily's colleagues at the university. With plates full of food provided by Callaloo and glasses of mulled wine and Bradford ale, the group toasted Emily and remanded her gentle soul to eternal peace.

EPILOGUE

Another winter passed and by early the following March all the snow melted in a rush, and weather-beaten grass again became visible in the yards and parks. A fierce windstorm, blowing in from the northwest towards the end of the month, had pushed tons of sand back from the crescent beach towards the small cottages that nestled behind the dune lines, creating a four-foot drop at the edge of the water.

Before the beach officially opened later that spring, crews of workers with front loaders would dredge up the sand and rebuild the beach to its original sloping contour, but for now, anyone wanting to walk directly along the shoreline had to jump over the steep embankment.

On a balmy morning in early April, just after the sun rose, Ed pulled Wellingtons onto his feet over his jeans, donned his windbreaker over a knitted jersey, and with his metal detector headed for the beach. He found a spot where the water had receded that was broad enough to do some exploring and began skimming his detector along the wet sand. Gentle waves rolled onto the shore, and screeching gulls circled above him in the sky.

On this piercingly clear day with the vivid sun casting sparkles of light that reflected like clear glass prisms onto the cerulean sea, and north towards the horizon, he believed he could see the curvature of the earth. Pearly freshwater oyster shells and small, smooth stones in muted colors of gray, green, tan and rust littered the sand.

As he strolled along the water's edge, his detector began to beep, and about five feet away he noticed something sticking up from beneath the sand. The beeping got louder as he got closer, and he saw the corner of a corroded metal box. Pulling a small shovel out of his pocket, he bent down and began to dig.

THE END

Annie DeCleryk's Recipes

As you may have noticed, Annie DeCleryk likes to cook. She graciously shared with us some of her recipes.

SPICY FISH CHOWDER

2 14.5 oz. cans chicken broth
2 ½ C. water
2/3 C. uncooked instant rice
1 ½ C. medium to hot jarred salsa
1 10 oz. package frozen corn
1 lb. frozen cod, thawed and cut into two-inch pieces
Fresh lime wedges, optional

In a large saucepan or Dutch oven, bring broth, water and rice to a boil. Reduce heat; cover and simmer for five minutes. Add the salsa and corn; return to a boil. Add fish. Reduce heat, cover and simmer for five minutes or until the fish flakes easily with a fork. Serve with lime, if desired. Serves 6-8.

COLESLAW WITH A TANGY OIL AND VINEGAR DRESSING

1 medium to large cabbage, shredded
2 medium carrots, shredded
1 small onion, diced
3 T. white Balsamic vinegar
1 T. Dijon mustard
3 T. extra virgin olive oil
1 tsp. dried cilantro, or 1 T. diced, fresh (optional)

Combine the cabbage, carrots and onion. Pour the vinegar into a small bowl and whisk the mustard into it.

In a slow stream, add the olive oil, whisking until the dressing is emulsified. Add the cilantro, if desired. Serves 6-8.

SHRIMP WITH FETA CHEESE AND TOMATOES

1 bunch green onions, diced or chopped
4 T. fresh, chopped parsley or about one Tbs. of dried
4 T. extra virgin olive oil
2 14.5 oz. cans Italian-style tomatoes, drained
Salt and pepper to taste
2 cloves garlic, minced (can also use dried garlic powder to taste)
1 C. clam juice or vegetable broth
2-3 lbs. frozen, cooked shrimp, tails removed
½ C. melted butter
½ C. dry white wine
1 T. dried oregano (or to taste)
8-12 oz. crumbled sheep's milk feta cheese

Preheat oven to 350 degrees. Cook green onions and parsley in oil in a hot skillet over medium heat, stirring constantly until onion is tender. Stir in tomatoes and next three ingredients; bring to a boil. Reduce heat and simmer for about five minutes so sauce becomes thickened. Add clam juice or stock to vegetable mixture and cook five more minutes. Pour mixture into a rectangular or oval baking dish.

Remove tails from frozen shrimp (no need to defrost or you can run shrimp under cold water). Spoon shrimp into baking dish over the tomato sauce and drizzle butter over shrimp and then sprinkle with wine, oregano and cheese. Bake in oven for 20-30 minutes until hot and bubbly. Serve with crusty French bread and a green salad. Serves 4-6. Recipe can be doubled or tripled.

TUSCAN TOMATO SOUP WITH GARLIC BREAD CROUTONS

1 loaf crusty Italian bread cut into 1" cubes
¼ C. extra virgin olive oil
¼ tsp. ground pepper
3 medium red onions, sliced ¼" thick
6 medium carrots, scrubbed and cut into large chunks
15 cloves garlic or jarred minced garlic measured to the equivalent
½ tsp. salt
5 C. prepared marinara sauce (about 1 ½ 24-oz. jars)
2 14.5 oz. cans low sodium chicken broth
1 ¼ C. hearty red wine
Preheat oven to 450 degrees.

Make croutons. Toss the bread with 2 T. oil and pepper in a large bowl. Spread the bread in a single layer on a baking sheet and toast 6-10 minutes until golden. Set aside.

Make the soup. Toss the onions, carrots, garlic, remaining olive oil and salt in a bowl. Spread vegetables on a baking pan and roast for about 10 minutes, turn and continue to roast until browned and soft- about 10 more minutes. Transfer vegetables to a bowl of a food processor fitted with a metal blade and pulse until finely chopped.

Combine marinara, broth and wine in a soup pot over medium heat and bring to a boil Reduce heat to medium-low and simmer, uncovered, for about five minutes. Add chopped vegetables, increase heat to medium and continue to simmer for 20 minutes. Stir in half the croutons and cook for five more minutes (soup will thicken). Place soup in bowls and garnish with reserved croutons. Serve immediately.

To freeze soup, prepare all steps as above. Ladle soup into freezer containers and put croutons in plastic freezer bags. When ready to serve, defrost and heat soup and follow step 5 above after soup is heated. Serves 6-8. Recipe can be doubled or tripled.

CHICKEN WITH FENNEL

One or two large fennel bulbs
14.5 oz. canned diced tomatoes, drained
¼ C. dry white wine
1T. grated orange zest
3 garlic cloves, minced
2 tsp. Balsamic vinegar
1/8 tsp. red pepper flakes
6 skinless, bone-in chicken breast halves (5 oz. each) or a combination of breasts and thighs
2 T. chopped Italian parsley

Cut the fennel bulbs into small wedges. In a non-stick frying pan sprayed with cooking spray (or you can use olive or canola oil), combine tomatoes, wine, orange zest, garlic, vinegar and pepper flakes. Cook over medium heat, stirring occasionally, until the mixture comes to a boil, then reduce heat to medium-low.

Arrange the chicken and fennel over the tomato mixture, spooning a bit of sauce over them. Cover and cook until chicken is opaque throughout and the fennel is tender, about 25 minutes. Transfer chicken to a platter, and increase heat to high and cook the sauce until it has thickened slightly.

At this point, if ready to serve you can spoon the sauce over the chicken and fennel and sprinkle with parsley or you can heat the sauce later and return the chicken to the pot and warm that way. Serves 4-6. Recipe and be doubled or tripled.

VEGETABLE CURRY IN A CROCKPOT

1 T. vegetable oil
2 large carrots, sliced on a diagonal
1 medium yellow onion, chopped
3 garlic cloves, minced
2 T. curry powder
1 tsp. ground coriander
¼ tsp. cayenne pepper
2 large, white or Yukon Gold potatoes, peeled and diced
8 oz. green beans, trimmed and cut into one-inch pieces
1 15.5 can chickpeas, drained and rinsed
1 15.5 oz.-can diced tomatoes, drained
2 C. vegetable stock
½ C. frozen peas
½ C. canned, unsweetened coconut milk, or to taste.

Heat oil over medium heat in a large skillet. Add carrots and onion and cook until softened, about five minutes. Add garlic, curry powder, coriander, and cayenne, stirring to coat.

Transfer vegetable mixture to a 3.5- to 4- quart slow cooker. Add potatoes, green beans, chickpeas, tomatoes, and stock and cook on Low setting for 6-8 hours.

Just before serving, stir in the peas and coconut milk, and if desired add salt and pepper to taste. Serves 4-6.

WHOLE-WHEAT IRISH SODA BREAD

1 ½ cups whole wheat pastry flour
1 ½ cups all-purpose flour
1 ½ tsp. baking soda
1 ½ tsp. salt
1 ¾ cups low-fat buttermilk

Preheat oven to 400-degrees, and line a large sheet pan with parchment paper. In a large bowl, combine flours, baking soda and salt; whisk to lighten and remove any lumps. Make a well in the center of the dry ingredients and pour in the buttermilk.

Gently mix with a rubber spatula until combined; do not knead or overwork the dough. Turn dough out onto prepared pan. Gently form into an even and round loaf and cut a shallow "x" pattern across the center using a serrated knife. Bake for 25 to 30 min or until firm and lightly golden. Allow to cool for 10 to 15 minutes before slicing. Makes one loaf, can be sliced into 12 large or 24 small slices.

FABULOUS CARAMELIZED VIDALIA ONION DIP

2 T. butter (use real stick butter and not margarine)
3 large Vidalia or other sweet onions thinly sliced
1 8 oz. package cream cheese softened (can use light or regular)
1 8 oz. block Swiss cheese, shredded (can use reduced fat)
1 C. freshly grated Parmesan cheese
1 C. regular or light mayonnaise
Sweet potato chips

Preheat oven to 375 degrees. Melt butter in a large skillet over medium heat; add sliced onions. Cook, stirring often, about 30-45 minutes or until onions are caramel-colored.

Combine onions with remaining ingredients, except sweet potato chips, and spoon into a lightly greased 1 ½ to 2-cup round baking dish. Bake uncovered for 30 minutes or until dip is golden and bubbly. Serve with sweet potato chips. Yields about 4 cups (enough for a group of six to ten depending on whether or not you are serving other hors' d'oeuvres).

Make ahead: Prepare dip a day ahead but do not bake. Cover and refrigerate overnight. Bake uncovered.

FLOURLESS CHOCOLATE TORTE

16 oz. semisweet baking chocolate squares, chopped
1 C. butter
2 T. coffee liqueur or 2 T. strong coffee
8 large eggs, separated
1 ½ C. sugar
Favorite chocolate sauce
Garnishes: whipped cream or whipped topping, fresh raspberries, blueberries and/or strawberries.

Combine chocolate and butter in a large heavy saucepan. Cook and stir over low heat until melted. Remove from heat, stir in liqueur and cool slightly.

Preheat oven to 350 degrees. Beat egg whites in a large mixing bowl at high speed with an electric beater until stiff peaks form. Beat egg yolks and sugar in another large mixing bowl at medium speed until thick and pale. Fold one-third of chocolate mixture into yolk mixture. Gently fold in one-third of egg whites. Fold in remaining chocolate mixture and egg whites. Pour batter into a greased and floured 10-inch spring form pan.

Bake at 350 degrees for 30 minutes or until edges are set (center will not be set). Remove from oven, and gently run a knife around edge of pan to release torte. Cool to room temperature on a wire rack; when cooled, cover and chill in refrigerator for 8 hours. Remove sides of pan just before serving. Serve with heated chocolate sauce and berries, if desired. Serves 12.

ABOUT THE AUTHOR

 Karen Shughart received a B.A. in Comprehensive Literature from the University of Pittsburgh and completed graduate courses in English at Shippensburg University.

She is the author of two non-fiction books, and has worked as an editor, publicist, photographer, journalist, teacher and non-profit executive. *Murder in the Museum: An Edmund DeCleryk Mystery* is her first work of fiction.

Before moving to a small village on the shores of Lake Ontario in upstate New York, she and her husband resided in south central Pennsylvania, near Harrisburg, PA. For more information, visit her website at: www.karenshughart.com.

Available now!

When a childhood friend of Ed DeCleryk is found murdered in a cemetery where the casualties of the War of 1812 are buried, Ed is hired to investigate. In book two of the series, *Murder in the Cemetery,* you'll learn what he found on the beach in *Murder in the Museum* and how that, and an artifact dating back to the early 1800s, are linked to this untimely death.

Made in the USA
Columbia, SC
23 August 2022

65151323R00159